'There isn't going to be any divorce! Not if I have any say in the matter, and certainly not before I've had a face-to-face meeting with Callie to find out why she's taken off like this.'

Con scrubbed his free hand over his face, wondering when he was ever going to get a good night's sleep again. It had been months, already, as he'd lain in the darkness beside Callie, listening to her toss and turn. He'd tried to comfort her in the days after she'd come out of hospital, but she'd still been totally overwhelmed by the disaster and, while she had often gravitated towards him in the brief hours when she slept, the rest of the time she had pushed him away—physically and mentally.

'Where *are* you, Callie?' he muttered aloud.

Josie Metcalfe lives in Cornwall with her long-suffering husband. They have four children. When she was an army brat, frequently on the move, books became the only friends that came with her wherever she went. Now that she writes them herself she is making new friends, and hates saying goodbye at the end of a book—but there are always more characters in her head, clamouring for attention until she can't wait to tell their stories.

Recent titles by the same author:

SHEIKH SURGEON, SURPRISE BRIDE
A FAMILY TO COME HOME TO
A VERY SPECIAL PROPOSAL

A MARRIAGE MEANT TO BE

BY
JOSIE METCALFE

MILLS & BOON™
Pure reading pleasure

All the characters in this book have no existence outside the imagination of the author, and have no relation whatsoever to anyone bearing the same name or names. They are not even distantly inspired by any individual known or unknown to the author, and all the incidents are pure invention.

First published in Great Britain 2007
Large Print edition 2007
Harlequin Mills & Boon Limited,
Eton House, 18-24 Paradise Road,
Richmond, Surrey TW9 1SR

© Josie Metcalfe 2007

ISBN: 978 0 263 19372 5

Set in Times Roman 16¾ on 19¾ pt.
17-1107-52895

Printed and bound in Great Britain
by Antony Rowe Ltd, Chippenham, Wiltshire

A MARRIAGE
MEANT TO BE

PROLOGUE

'WHAT on *earth's* wrong with Con?' demanded one of the junior nurses as she entered the staffroom.

'Sue and I just saw him in the car park and said hello,' said her companion as she shrugged out of her coat, 'but he walked straight past us without a word…and he looks *dreadful*.'

'Haven't you heard?' someone said in hushed tones that still somehow managed to carry to everyone in the room. 'Callie lost their baby…a stillbirth.'

'No! Oh, she must be devastated!' Sue said with a gasp of dismay. 'It's taken them so long to get pregnant, and just when everyone thought it was all going to be fine this time…'

'Only the other day I overheard Con teasing her about how much the baby was kicking. He said something about this one being the start of their five-a-side football team,' someone else piped up. 'Why do such rotten things happen to such nice people? The two of them would be wonderful parents.'

'To say nothing about what gorgeous children they'd produce,' said another. 'They're both slim and elegant-looking and they've both got that beautiful dark hair. The only toss-up would be whether the kids got his blue eyes or her grey ones.'

'How long will it be before they can start another round of IVF?' Sue asked the room at large.

'Months, I expect,' her friend said grimly. 'They'll probably have to wait for her body to recover from the pregnancy before they can try again.'

'That's if they can face going through it another time,' a fresh voice said coolly. 'It must be frustrating for him to know that he's firing on all cylinders and could have had his football team by now if he were married to someone else.'

With that comment there was a distinct change in the atmosphere of the staff room—a sour note that hadn't been there before—and it wasn't long before everyone was hurrying off in their different directions, leaving the nurse who had made the comment all alone.

'Well, I was only saying aloud what everyone else knows,' she muttered, tight-lipped. 'He's a good-looking man in a good job with the prospect of being made consultant in the not-too-distant future. Of course he wants a family…and a wife who can give him that family.'

She turned towards the mirror, watching herself with a calculating smile as she fluffed her blonde hair around her face.

CHAPTER ONE

'WHERE are *you*, Callie?' Con muttered aloud, his concern increasing by the second as he put the phone down again. 'What on earth's happened to you?'

It wasn't like her to let people down like this. She should have turned up for her shift nearly two hours ago, and it didn't matter how many times he'd tried to contact her, there had been no answer, not at home or on her mobile.

'Con, can you come and have a look at Mrs Fry for me?' said an all-too-familiar voice at his elbow, and he sighed, dragging his fingers through his hair with frustration.

'Isn't there anyone else free, Sonja?' he asked as he turned to face the willowy blonde nurse who seemed determined to dog his every step these days. 'I'm trying to make some phone calls.'

'She's an elderly lady who's had a fall,' Sonja said earnestly, clutching his arm with a determined hand. 'She's obviously broken both wrists but it's the wound on her head I'm worried about. She must have hit it pretty hard to gash it like that. We've stemmed the bleeding but she seems very confused. I need to know whether she should go for an MRI.'

He sighed again, knowing he was going to have to look at the poor lady, even though his concern for Callie was growing by the minute.

'Which cubicle is she in?' he asked, resigned to the few minutes' delay before he could contact their neighbour.

Jan should be home any minute if she'd followed her usual routine of doing her shopping when she finished her shift, and he was certain she wouldn't mind going next door for him. If there was no answer, she had an emergency key to let herself in. If Callie had been taken ill or had some sort of accident that prevented her getting to the phone…

'Thank you for doing this for me,' Sonja gushed, and he rolled his eyes behind her back as he followed her along the corridor. Sycophancy was something he'd never been able to stomach, especially when he had too much else on his mind…like his precious, vulnerable Callie.

'Hello, Mrs Fry. I'm one of the doctors here. What have you been doing to yourself?' Even as he approached the elderly lady his eyes were beginning their primary survey, noting how pale and shaky she was and wondering how much of that was normal for her.

'I fell coming in from the hens,' she quavered, peering up at him from under the bulk of a pressure bandage wound tightly around her head. 'Hit my head and broke both my eggs.'

'No, dear, it wasn't your *legs* you broke; it was your *wrists*,' Sonja corrected in the annoyingly bright tone some people adopted with children and the elderly.

Con threw her a quelling glare and turned back to the little woman who seemed far from confused to him, despite her age and the recent trauma.

'*Eggs*,' the woman repeated stubbornly, fixing her pale blue gaze on Con. 'I'd been out to the hens and was bringing the eggs back into the house when I missed the step.'

'Ouch!' Con said sympathetically, as he took a peep under the bandage and saw the size of the gash on her forehead. He wouldn't disturb it too much until it was time to stitch it, not while the newly formed clots were slowing the bleeding to a sluggish seep. 'There was one step you *should* have missed. Are you in a lot of pain?'

'I'm eighty-two, doctor. At my age I'm always in pain. Everything's wearing out.'

'What about your hands? Can you move your fingers for me?' he asked, as he pressed on a nail bed of each hand to check that her circulation wasn't being compromised by the broken bones.

'I can, but I don't want to because they hurt,' she said with a stubborn glint in her eyes.

Con grinned at her. 'If I give you something to take the pain away, will you move them for me?'

'I might,' she conceded. 'But when can I go

home? The ambulance people wouldn't let me clean the broken eggs off the step. It'll be a terrible job to do if it dries on. *And* they shut my dogs Floss and Nell in the kitchen. They'll be needing to go out to do their business.'

'You won't be able to go home for a little while, Mrs Fry,' he said gently, delaying the moment he'd probably have to tell her that she was going to have to be admitted. With two broken wrists most people would need help to take care of themselves, let alone an eighty-two-year-old with chickens and two dogs to take care of. 'First, we need to take some pictures. Then we can sort out your hands and fix the cut on your head.'

'But how soon can I go home?' she demanded, clearly determined to get an answer. 'I haven't even given the dogs their breakfast, yet.'

'Have *you* had anything to eat this morning?' he sidestepped, not wanting to upset her with the bad news until he knew exactly what they were dealing with.

He quickly scrawled his signature on the paperwork for an MRI of her head to rule out any injury to her brain and X-rays of both wrists to find out exactly how many breaks there were in there. Depending on what each revealed, the poor woman might even have to go to Theatre for Orthopaedics to patch her up.

'Haven't eaten anything yet. *That's* why I was out getting the eggs. I was going to boil one and have it with some toast—I still make all my own bread,' she added with a spark of pride, 'and my own marmalade, too.'

Con's stomach gave a sudden noisy growl and he chuckled. 'You can't imagine just how delicious that all sounds at this time of the morning,' he said, even as his thoughts automatically flew to Callie and the way she always insisted on setting a place at the table for him before she came out to work. There would be no breakfast for him any time soon—not until she turned up to start her shift. They were far too short-staffed during this early-morning rush of patients for him to feel comfortable taking off just because it was past the end of his own shift. As long as the department manager didn't spot him…

'Dr Lowell! Your shift ended two hours ago,' said a stern voice behind him as he was making for the nearest phone, and he turned with a rueful grin to meet the unsmiling eyes of Selina Drew.

She wasn't a big woman by anybody's standards but there was absolutely no question about who ruled St Mark's A and E department.

'I know, Selina, but—'

'But nothing! There's no point thinking you can soft-soap me,' she continued firmly. 'You had a tough shift last night and you know as well as I do that you won't be able to do your job properly when you come on shift again if you don't get a proper rest.'

She was right, but under the circumstances…

'I wasn't just staying on for the fun of it,' he said, uncomfortably aware that there was definitely a defensive sound to his voice. And he was tired…oh, so tired. Sometimes it felt as if the weariness had penetrated right to the marrow of his bones. 'Callie hasn't arrived yet, and I was just…' He shrugged.

'You were just keeping busy while you waited

for her to turn up?' she suggested kindly, obviously understanding far more of his situation that he'd realised. 'Well, Con, as of this moment, you're officially off the clock. I've just been informed by the office that your wife's reported off sick today. Now, get yourself home and take care of each other.'

She started to turn away from him then changed her mind.

'How is Callie *really* doing, Con?' she asked, and with this lion-hearted woman he knew that the question came out of genuine concern rather than any other reason. 'It's just that…well, she seemed to be coping reasonably well since she came back to work, right until the last few days.'

Con blinked, puzzled. 'What do you mean? What's been happening the last few days? I didn't know she'd been having problems. She hasn't said anything to me.'

'Not problems, exactly.' She pulled a face, looking as if she now regretted saying anything. 'It's almost as though… as though she's had something weighing on her mind. You know how it is when you're trying to make a decision about something?'

'Did she give you any idea what it was about?' he asked.

It didn't feel quite right to be pumping Selina for information, but if there was something that Callie was worrying about—something that was actually affecting the way she did her job— then it was something he needed to know about. They'd spent the last three years going through hell and high water together as they'd tried to start a family the hard way, and he couldn't believe that there was *anything* they couldn't talk about any more.

'I was going to ask you the same thing,' she admitted, then paused a second as though worried about encroaching on private territory. 'Con, I didn't know if perhaps the two of you were trying to make a decision about calling a halt...if you'd decided that she'd been through enough?'

He closed his eyes and sighed, pressing his head back against the wall, knowing that if he didn't consciously keep his knees locked he would probably slide right down into a heap on the floor.

When he was busy, he could almost forget, but as soon as the memories surfaced, the devastation was enough to cut him off at the knees. He could only guess how much worse it was for Callie. The first two pregnancies hadn't even progressed far enough to show, and she'd broken her heart over each of them. The third one—third time lucky, they'd told each other as the weeks had gone past—had been more than halfway to term when the routine ultrasound had failed to pick up a heartbeat and they'd learned that the baby had died before they'd even held him.

'I tried to talk about it the other day,' he murmured, feeling the warmth of her concern as she stood silently beside him. 'Because we just can't go on in…in limbo like this, but she said she just wasn't ready yet. You know this one was just such a shock…'

He couldn't go on. His eyes were already burning with the threat of tears when he remembered the tiny boy she'd finally given birth to after six hours of induced agony, and how perfect he'd looked in every way. It still tore his heart out by the roots to think that his son would never open his eyes or smile or walk, that his precious life had been over before it had begun.

'Go home, Con,' Selina said with a gentle pat on his arm. 'If she hasn't turned up at work this morning it's because she's still at home and she needs you with her. Just one thing, though. If the two of you need an extra day or two to get your heads on straight, let me know so I don't end up without any staff at all! I'll need some time to call in favours.'

'Will do, boss!' he said with a flip of a salute, suddenly eager to get home. He had no idea why Callie wasn't answering her mobile phone—unless she'd forgotten to charge the battery again—but Selina was probably right. He'd get home and she would be sitting in the kitchen-diner they'd remodelled together with a pot of coffee and a pile of freshly made toast…no, make that a scattering of crumbs on the plate, because she wouldn't have sat there looking at hot buttered toast for long without tucking in.

And while she was waiting, she'd be going over in her head exactly what she wanted to say, and as soon as he walked in she would stand there and deliver her little prepared speech the way she always did once she'd weighed everything up and come to a decision….

And all the while he was driving, a little corner of his brain was doing calculations and lining up facts and figures, deliberately cross-checking the tests he'd ordered on the patients he'd seen…anything to stop him trying to second-guess what she was going to say. After all, it was her body so ultimately it was her decision whether to put it through yet another round of IVF…or whether to finally abandon the attempt at having the child she desperately wanted.

The short distance to the spacious home they'd bought when they'd first got married— chosen both for its proximity to the hospital and because they'd thought they would have no problem filling it with children—was long enough for him to recall that it was nearly five months since their son had been stillborn.

In that time they'd both spent far too many nights staring into the darkness, alone with their thoughts even though they still shared the same room and the same bed they always had. Yet, in spite of that surface closeness, in all those weeks he'd been very careful not to let Callie know how much he'd missed the ultimate intimacy of making love with her, their joining not just the sexual one of bodies but of hearts, minds and spirits, too. He'd been determined to wait until she was ready, but she'd only ever shown that she would welcome his attentions once, and with his emotions on a hair trigger with the months of abstinence, that had hardly been an outstanding success.

He'd hoped that his consideration would help to show her how much he cared for her but now he wondered if it might have been a mistake to put a lid on what he was thinking, how he was feeling and what he wanted. If she'd spent all that time waiting for *him* to make the first move…

He chuckled wryly when he realised that was all too possible. He had been Callie's first and only lover, and while she was a generous and passionate woman she still remained a little shy about letting him know what she liked and how she liked it when they came together.

'Let's hope that today marks the start of a new beginning,' he said with an expectant lift to his spirits. Selina had seemed to think that Callie had been coming to a decision about something over the last few days, but what that decision was, he had absolutely no idea.

The thought of abandoning that last batch of fertilised eggs to their liquid nitrogen prison put a lump in his throat that threatened to choke him. She'd been so adamant that she wanted the children she carried to be *their* babies that she'd put herself through misery over and over again before she'd managed to produce enough viable ova.

But, ultimately, it was her choice. *Her* body would have to go through the punishing hormone regimen to prepare it for implantation, and they knew to their cost that getting pregnant wasn't anywhere near the end of the road.

'Whatever she's decided will be OK with me,' he said firmly as he pulled into the driveway, puzzled to see that she'd put her car away in the garage rather than leaving it in the drive ready to go to work. 'Callie is what matters more than anything. She's my wife and I love her. No one has an absolute right to have children. We have a good, strong relationship and a happy marriage, so a family would have just been a wonderful bonus.'

There was still the possibility of adoption, with so many children needing loving homes, but even though Callie might still be desperate for a child, it might take a while longer before she was ready to contemplate that step. For now, it was time to sit down together and talk…*really* talk…and to repair and strengthen the bonds that had made the two of them invincible.

'Callie?' he called as soon as he let himself into the house, feeling more upbeat than he had in a very long time. 'Sweetheart? Where are you?'

The silence almost echoed around him with a strangely ominous feeling.

'Callie?' He could hear the sharper edge to his voice this time as his feet took him swiftly down the polished hallway along the original floorboards that they'd laboriously refinished. A quick glance in either direction as he passed the open doors told him that she wasn't in the lounge or the spacious study they shared, or in the formal dining room they only used when they were entertaining.

'Sweetheart?' He pushed the kitchen door wide and shuddered when he took in the almost clinical neatness of the whole room. Every surface gleamed and there wasn't even a teaspoon on the work surface where she always made her last cup of instant coffee before she left the house each day. There certainly wasn't any evidence of hot buttered toast.

Panic roared through him and in an instant he was racing back down the hall and taking the stairs two and even three at a time in his desperate need to get to their bedroom and the *en suite* bathroom.

'She *wouldn't*,' he told himself fiercely, fighting with a sudden nightmare vision of his wife's lifeless body sprawled across their bed or on the bathroom floor.

It was a heart-stopping body blow to realise that he might have drifted that far away from her. He honestly didn't know if she'd become so depressed that she might attempt suicide, but he prayed that her deep reverence for life would have prevented her taking that awful step.

'Oh, thank you, God,' he whispered as he clung to the doorframe, tears of relief already starting to flow when he realised that she wasn't there...wasn't anywhere in the house, in fact.

It took him several minutes to compose himself and a cold facecloth to remove the evidence of his loss of control before he dragged his heavy feet across to slump on the side of the bed.

'So, where are you, sweetheart? Where have you gone?' he asked the silent room, with a sudden memory of the laughter that had filled it when they'd been decorating it together, getting more paint on each other than the walls and then having to spend ages under the shower washing each other off...just to be certain there were no spots of paint remaining, of course.

His eyes drifted across to the photograph in the silver frame that graced the dressing-table, searching out the bright, laughing face he loved so much…and found it covered by the envelope propped against it with his own name written across it in her familiar script.

Dread wrapped around his heart as he reached for it, his hand visibly trembling as he pulled the single sheet of paper out and fumbled to unfold it.

There was no heading to the letter. No 'Dear Con', 'Darling' or 'My Love', the way she always began the most mundane of notes. Before he could even focus on what she'd written his heart was breaking to see the marks on the paper where her tears had fallen.

'I'm sorry it's taken me so long to admit that I'll never be able to give you what you want,' she said in the frighteningly brief missive. *'It's best if I go away so you can start the divorce proceedings. Let Martin know what you want to do. I won't fight it. Be happy.'*

'No!' he roared in disbelief. 'Callie, no!' And he felt his heart shatter in agony.

* * *

Callie turned her face to the window as the woman beside her got out of her seat and set off to leave the coach, the bulging photo album detailing every moment of her grandchildren's lives back safely in her handbag.

She rested her head against the glass, hoping that her next companion on this never-ending journey would take the hint and leave her alone with her thoughts.

She didn't want to know about anyone else's problems. She only wanted to know how she was going to cope with her own…how she was going to find the will to draw her next breath when she'd just walked away from everything she'd ever loved.

Not that it had been an easy decision, far from it. In fact, she was ashamed to realise how selfish she'd been for so long, wasting years and an almost obscene amount of money trying to force her body to do something it would never be able to manage—give them the child they'd both wanted.

She tried to stop the image forming inside her

head but it was already there, indelibly, for the rest of her life.

The tears began again as she remembered how grey and still her baby had been when he'd finally been born.

He'd been perfect. Absolutely perfect in every way, with ten tiny fingers and toes each with the most minute nail already there and growing. She would never know whether he'd inherited Con's deep blue eyes or her own grey ones or whether he would have the mischievous dimples that punctuated her husband's cheeks whenever he smiled.

Not that he'd been smiling much in the last four months and twenty-three days. It seemed as if they'd both forgotten how to do that when they'd seen that precious little image on the screen and realised that the heart had no longer been beating.

The memory was still so painful that she could barely draw breath, her own heart feeling as though some alien force was crushing it inside her chest. What right did it have to beat when her baby's didn't? Why was it that even the youngest teenage girl could manage to get pregnant, seemingly with even the most meaningless of sexual encounters, while she…she couldn't carry a child for the man she'd loved from the first moment their eyes had met, the only man she'd ever loved.

No more crying, she told herself, suddenly remembering that she mustn't do anything to draw too much attention to herself. *Concentrate on something else*—except there wasn't much else to look at in the barren wasteland of a bus and coach depot other than the people in the queue waiting to get on.

She hastily dragged her eyes away from the young woman struggling to fold up her baby's pushchair single-handed with the child cradled in the other arm. She wouldn't allow herself so much as a glimpse of the perfect little face so she would have no idea if it was a girl or a boy, if it was about the same age that *her*…

No! Concentrate on the two girls chattering brightly together. Were they friends setting off for a day's shopping in the next big town or was this just the most convenient way for them to get to and from work each day?

The two older women in front of them were talking equally animatedly. Were they friends taking the trip together or were each of them like her previous garrulous companion, lucky to have found someone equally inclined to chat?

And the cadaverous young man with the tattoo sprawling up one side of his grubby neck? It was all too easy after spending time as an A and E doctor to spot the fact that he was a drug addict, but whether he was using illegal Class A drugs or had gone onto a methadone programme was more difficult to tell at first glance. The ravages of what he'd been doing to his body weren't.

Then, in front of him, there was the white-faced young woman obviously trying hard not to cry as the stern-faced man spoke to her through a mouth thinned by a mixture of anger and exasperation. It must be hard for him to keep his voice down so the rest of the queue couldn't hear what he was saying. He looked like the sort of man used to having his orders obeyed without question.

Apparently unaware that the passengers

already on the bus had a bird's-eye view of those waiting to join them, the man took out his wallet and grabbed several high-denomination bills, folding them twice, neatly, before he tried to press them into the girl's hand.

Initially, she refused to take them, shaking her head fiercely, and the revulsion on her face was a far clearer indication of what was happening than any words she was saying. But, of course, the older man had made up his mind and with a few terse words denied her objections and thrust the money into her hand before he abruptly turned on his heel and strode away.

And then it was time for them to board and Callie watched out of the corner of her eye to see where each of them ended up.

Thankfully, the young woman with the baby decided to sit somewhere near the front. Callie didn't know if she could have borne it if she'd chosen to sit beside her for the next hour or two. She wouldn't have been able to resist the temptation of looking and longing and…

The two young women chattered their way towards the back of the coach, leaving a trail of perfume in their wake, unlike the cadaverous young man. She was uncomfortably aware of holding her breath as he stood for several seconds beside the empty seat next to her, but he, too, passed on down the coach.

It was the white-faced young woman who finally slid herself into place beside her and it was only then that Callie saw what hadn't been visible while the youngster had been part of the queue. She was pregnant.

Callie drew in a sharp breath as the shock hit her, and closed her eyes while she battled against the jealous tears with the realisation that she seemed to be showing about the same as *she* had, just before…

'It's not catching, you know,' the young woman snapped with an attempt at bravado that was completely destroyed by the wobble in her voice.

'Unfortunately,' Callie muttered, even as she felt guilt that her reaction had made the young woman feel uncomfortable.

'You…what?' Her garishly painted mouth fell open and eyes heavily outlined with kohl grew wide. 'Did you say…unfortunately?'

'Yes,' Callie admitted uncomfortably, wishing she'd either kept her mouth shut or stuck to a simple apology for her apparent disapproval. Now she was going to have to make some sort of explanation even though she knew it was going to hurt more than ripping a scab off a wound that had barely started healing. 'I lost my baby nearly five months ago. I was just over halfway through the pregnancy.'

'Oh…! I'm sorry if it makes you… Look, would you rather I asked someone else to swap seats with me?' she asked earnestly, revealing a far more considerate side than the initial belligerent attitude would have suggested.

There was a sudden rumble of sound as the driver started the engine and an explosive hiss of air as he released the brakes to start the next stage of the journey.

'It's too late now,' Callie said, resigned to a companion who was managing, in her early teens, to do what she, a mature professional, couldn't do with all the expertise of her health service colleagues behind her. 'You can't go changing seats while the coach is moving. If the driver had to brake suddenly you might injure the baby if you hit something.'

The youngster stared at her in surprise then she pressed trembling lips together and Callie was startled to see that her eyes were swimming with tears.

'I'm sorry. Did I say something to upset you?' Callie was suddenly concerned that she must have inadvertently hit a sensitive nerve.

'No. It's just… You said that as if you actually care what happens to it…to the baby,' she said in a choked voice.

'Of course I do. Anybody would,' Callie said, knowing that this wasn't the time to talk about her own desperate longing for a child.

'Not everybody,' she snapped bitterly, then suddenly seemed to remember that they were surrounded on all sides and lowered her voice so that her words would be masked by the sound of the other voices around them and the rumble of the coach itself. 'My stepfather gave me money for an abortion even though he knows it's too far along. He said if you pay enough money any doctor would do it.'

'Most doctors wouldn't touch it with a bargepole even if you offered them the moon on a silver platter,' Callie said quietly. In her days on Obs and Gyn she'd seen botched abortions go horribly wrong. 'And why would you want to abort the baby when there are so many people desperate to adopt?'

'I don't *want* to give it away,' she said fiercely, a protective hand curving over her noticeably swollen belly even as she lost her battle with the tears. 'But I've got no way of keeping it, have I? Not at my age. I'm still at school and a Saturday job won't pay enough to find somewhere to live.'

'What about your mum? Won't she help you?'

'Not her!' she said, bitterness and devastation combining corrosively in those two words. 'She kicked me out when she found out. She would have killed me if she knew it was *his*…my stepfather's.'

Callie thought it would have been more to the point if the mother had killed the stepfather who'd been having sex with her underage daughter, but now wasn't the time to voice those sentiments. She fished a packet of paper hankies out of her pocket and offered them to her companion.

'Listen, we're going to be sitting together for at least an hour. Shall we introduce ourselves? I'm Callie,' she said, holding out her hand.

'Steph…Stephanie,' she said, and blew her nose furiously. 'I didn't want to cry, not over them.'

'Hey, don't knock crying. Sometimes it's good to let some of the emotions out.'

'It doesn't solve anything, though—like, what am I going to do when the coach arrives at the depot? I've got nowhere to go and no one to ask.'

'That makes two of us,' Callie said, surprising herself.

'You…*what*?' Steph blinked. 'You're kidding! You're a grown-up and grown-ups always know where they're going and what they're going to do.'

'Newsflash, Steph. Grown-ups are just as mixed up as anybody else. They've just had a bit more practice at hiding it.'

CHAPTER TWO

'So, where do we go?' Steph said when the two of them had been reunited with their luggage.

Callie almost smiled when she realised that they had both opted for almost identical rucksacks in which to carry their worldly belongings.

'First, we need to find somewhere to stay the night,' Callie said, looking out at the rapidly darkening sky beyond the enormous doorway to the coach terminus. They'd managed to outrun the threatened bad weather so far, but it didn't look as if it would be long before they'd get soaked if they hadn't found somewhere. '*That* might be a good place to start,' she suggested, pointing to the internet café on the other side of the road.

'Uh, I don't think the café will stay open all night,' Steph said uneasily. 'I've got a bit of money to find a cheap hotel or something. I told you my stepfather gave it to me for the abortion but I reckon it was a bribe, too, so I wouldn't tell Mum it's his.'

Callie chuckled. 'I'm far too old to want to spend the night sitting in a café,' she said. 'I was actually going to go on the internet and see what I can find around here without having to march up and down in the dark.'

'You can do that?' Steph marvelled with all the arrogance of the very young for those they consider too 'past it' to cope with modern technology, and Callie suddenly felt as old as Methuselah's grandmother.

'Let's find out,' she suggested, and they set off into the chilly evening.

They reached the other said of the road and Callie was just stretching out a hand to open the door when there was the sound of running feet approaching. Before she could even shout a warning their malodorous fellow passenger had barged into Steph, sending her slamming into the pavement as he made off with her rucksack.

'*Steph!* Are you all right?' Callie demanded,

as she dropped to her knees beside the dazed youngster.

'Callie…?' she quavered, clearly shocked. 'What…? My bag!' she gasped, and started to struggle against Callie's hold. 'It's got all my money in it.'

'Steph, stay still!' she warned. 'You hit your head pretty hard when you went down. Let me check you over before—'

'But he's stolen my bag,' she insisted. 'He's getting away.'

'Sweetheart, he's gone. We'll never find him,' Callie said gently, while she held both of Steph's shoulders to try to stop her from moving. 'Now, please, let me check your head to see if there's any damage.'

Perhaps it was the calm insistence in her voice that finally got through the young girl's distress, but with tears already leaking out of the corner of her eyes and running into the too-black hair she stared up at Callie with a beaten expression in her eyes.

'Oh, Callie… What am I going to do now?' she whispered.

Behind them Callie heard the shop door open and looked back over her shoulder to see a gangling young man looking down at them.

'I saw what happened and phoned for an ambulance. The police are on their way, too,' he said. 'Should I make her a cup of tea? That's supposed to be good for shock, isn't it?'

'Thanks for making the call to the emergency services, but it's better not to give her anything to eat or drink until she's been checked out, just in case anything's broken,' Callie explained, as she performed a swift primary survey.

It was light enough, there on the pavement where the lights from the shop shone brightly, to see that Steph's pupils were equal and reactive to light and she didn't seem to have broken anything. There was a painful place where the back of her head had met the ground and the start of a goose egg, but she didn't even seem to have broken the skin, let alone be losing any untoward fluids.

'Can you remember what happened to you?' she asked gently, and Steph threw her an old-fashioned look.

'Callie, I haven't got concussion or amnesia. I've been mugged and had all my stuff nicked and I'm all alone in a city I've never visited before with nowhere to stay for the night. Oh, and I can remember the date *and* who's the prime minister.'

Callie chuckled when she saw the face Steph pulled. 'Not your type?' she teased. 'Well, I don't think you've done yourself any major damage, but for the baby's sake I think you ought to be checked over in the hospital.'

'Hospital!' she wailed over the sound of an approaching ambulance. 'I don't need to go there, do I? You said you couldn't find anything wrong.'

'Hey, Steph, look on the bright side. In the hospital it'll be warm and dry and they'll give you a bed to lie on.'

'Hey, classic!' she scoffed wearily. 'I get mugged and lose all my money so I can't afford even a cheap hotel but, gee, guess what? The mugger injures me so I get a bed for the night.'

Callie hoped her smile was reassuring but when she went to step aside to allow the paramedic to do his job Steph grabbed for her hand and held on tightly.

'You won't leave me, will you? Not until…' Her face fell as she suddenly realised that she had no idea what was going to happen to her.

Callie's heart went out to her, especially when she heard the tremor in her voice when she was answering the handsome young paramedic's questions.

'I'll stay with you if you want me to,' she offered, giving her hand a squeeze. 'I haven't got anywhere else I need to be in a hurry.' Nowhere she needed to be for the rest of her life, if the truth be told.

'Are you sure?' Steph asked, seeming painfully young in her insecurity; definitely not old enough to be thrown out to fend for herself in a strange city.

'I'm sure these nice young men won't mind if I come for a ride with you,' she said firmly, meeting the eyes of Mike, the good-looking young paramedic, with an authority learned the hard way during many hours of duty in a busy hospital A and E department. 'Especially given the fact that you're pregnant. They like pregnant mums to be calm and happy.'

'We certainly do, Stephanie,' he said with a broad smile, generously taking the hint without an argument. 'So you just settle yourself back and enjoy the ride in our luxury limousine.'

'Limousine!' she scoffed with a dismissing glance around the functional interior. 'Where's the plush carpeting and the mini-bar?'

'Hey, don't knock it,' Mike protested. 'I cleaned that floor myself, just before we came out to get you, and we've got lots of things in here that you don't get in a mini-bar—such as oxygen on tap.' He gently adjusted the mask over her face as he teased her and Callie could already see some of Steph's tension easing.

Her own anxiety had reduced the moment she'd seen how competent the ambulance crew was. Now she just needed to be certain that neither her young travelling companion nor her unborn baby had suffered any hidden injuries and she could go on her way.

Except she couldn't really do that with a clear conscience, knowing that Steph was now without any funds whatever. Yes, she would have a free bed for the night, tonight, but after that? What resources were there for underage pregnant girls in this city? Were there any hostels or refuges? The ideal situation would be a purpose-built home where she could stay while she waited out the rest of her pregnancy, preferably with counsellors available to tell her about the options available to help her to decide whether to keep her baby or give it up for adoption.

Perhaps she would be able to find out that sort of information while she waited for the A and E staff to check Steph over. She spared a longing thought for St Mark's, where such local gems had been collated onto the hospital database so that it would be readily to hand. Unfortunately, neither she nor Stephanie would be going back to that area again, at least not for the foreseeable future.

'Right, ladies, hold tight and we'll be on our way,' the driver called as he started the powerful engine.

Callie sat herself out of the way and put her

rucksack on her lap, wrapping both arms around it as she watched the paramedic check Steph's vital signs again and note his findings on the case notes he'd started.

'Just a few questions, Stephanie. The usual things, all right?' he said with pen poised. 'I need your name, address, date of birth and the name of your next of kin so we can notify them where we've taken you.'

Callie saw the youngster's tension return full force.

'My name's Stephanie…Smith and I'm fifteen,' she said tersely.

'And?' Mike encouraged, even though it was obvious she'd given a false surname.

'And I've got no address and no family to notify,' she said with a stubborn expression on her face that told Callie it would be useless to try to push her any further. The paramedic threw her a concerned glance over Steph's head but he obviously thought the same thing if his resigned sigh was anything to go by.

'Stephanie, that can cause problems for us,' he said gently.

'Why should it? I can take care of myself,' she said belligerently.

'You probably can,' he agreed, 'but according to the law, if you're under sixteen we have to have the permission of a parent or guardian to treat you.'

'That's easy, then. Just stop the ambulance and I'll get out, then you won't have to worry about getting sued.'

'Steph, sweetheart…' Callie began, not really knowing what to say. She'd often had to start treating youngsters before she could get parental consent—a victim of a car crash or a child in status asthmaticus couldn't wait for paperwork. Hopefully, Steph's condition wasn't life-threatening, but if it were…from the little that the youngster had told her on the coach, she was feeling too bitter at the moment to be willing to contact her family, and without a surname there was no way of tracking them down behind her back.

But if the alternative was watching a fifteen-year-old with a potential head injury disappear onto the streets without a penny to her name…

She unzipped a pocket on her rucksack and fished out the purse buried deep inside, out of the way of light-fingered passers-by.

'Here. Will this help with the paperwork?' she asked as she offered her hospital ID card.

She saw Mike's eyebrows shoot up when he read it and was uncomfortably aware that in her jeans and jumper she didn't look much like the professional photo he was looking at. But apart from that speculative look in her direction he confined himself to copying the relevant information on Steph's form.

'A and E,' their driver announced cheerfully, although Callie would have bet that he'd been listening to every word going on in the back and would be grilling Mike later.

'We hope you enjoyed your journey,' he said as he opened the double doors at the back of the vehicle, sounding just like a holiday tour guide, 'but sincerely hope you won't be travelling with us again.'

'Tony, you idiot,' scolded one of the nursing staff waiting to receive them. 'What have you brought for us this time?'

'Two lovely ladies,' he announced cheerfully, as he and Mike flipped the lock to release the wheels and slid the trolley smoothly out onto the apron and through the doors of the emergency department with Callie in their wake.

'This is Stephanie,' Mike said as soon as his hands were free to consult his clipboard. 'She's fifteen years old and approximately twenty-eight weeks gestational. She was mugged and fell, hitting her head on the pavement. Brief loss of consciousness but her obs are now all within normal ranges with pupils equal and reactive. No obvious breaks but the start of a lovely big egg on the back of her head.'

'Are you her mother?' the young nurse demanded, and Callie was so taken aback by the unexpected question that she hadn't managed a word before Steph butted in.

'No. She's my friend,' she announced fiercely, reaching for Callie's hand and clinging to it. 'She was there when it happened and I want her to stay with me.'

'That won't be a problem as long as she doesn't get in the way,' the young nurse said kindly, and

Mike had to stifle a chuckle when he caught Callie's eye. He opened his mouth, obviously intending to tell the team about her qualifications, but Callie gave her head a sharp shake, hoping he would keep the information to himself. Now was not the time to end up answering an inquisition about why she was so far from home.

She was also feeling overwhelmed by such familiar surroundings, having trouble coping with the fact that even though everything was so similar to St Mark's, there was one huge difference—there was no chance of coming out of the cubicle and seeing Con's familiar figure walking towards her with that sexy smile deepening the dimples either side of his mouth.

Not that she'd seen much of that sexy smile over the last few weeks and months. She hadn't felt much like smiling, either, but in her case it had been because she'd been mourning the death of the baby that would have made her life complete. She'd thought Con had been mourning, too. It had taken blunt words to open her eyes to the true state of affairs between them.

A very junior registrar came in a few minutes later and was doing very well until he caught sight of what Mike had written on Steph's case notes. Suddenly he became all fingers and thumbs and started second-guessing himself over every little thing until Callie couldn't stand it any more.

'I'll just go out and make a call while you're organising the ultrasound scan, shall I?' she suggested, taking pity on the poor man's nerves.

'You won't go away, will you, Callie?' Steph demanded, looking younger than ever swathed in a voluminous hospital gown.

'I promise,' Callie said with an encouraging smile. 'But I need to do something about my accommodation. We aren't *all* getting free beds for the night.'

'But you will come back, won't you?' she said, sounding as uncertain as a little child left for the first time in an unfamiliar place, but clearly hoping that no one would be able to hear the pleading in her voice.

'As soon as I've made my calls,' Callie reassured her, and slipped out of the cubicle.

'Can you direct me to a phone I can use to call out of the hospital?' she asked one of the women at the reception desk, having chosen her for the kindly way she'd spoken to the last person to approach her. 'And do you have any sort of directory of organisations in this area who provide sheltered accommodation for runaways or pregnant girls?'

The woman blinked at the question, but Callie would have to give her points for the fact that her smile never wavered neither did her eyes stray towards Callie's waistline.

'I've got some telephone numbers on a database on the computer. I could call them for you, or would you like me to print them out?'

'Could you print them out, please? Until my friend has finished having her tests, she won't know when she'll be released.'

'I wouldn't wait till then before you make contact,' she advised softly, as the printer started chattering, beckoning Callie to the far end of the reception desk to give them some semblance of privacy for their conversation. 'There's an excellent YMCA but they're always so heavily over-subscribed and only take people in on a night-by-night basis, so there's no continuity. There's only one official residential centre in town, and that takes the girls up to six weeks after the birth, so they rarely have any beds free.' She paused a moment in thought then wrote something on the paper. 'This one I'm adding at the bottom of the list is still trying to start up at the moment—they're struggling financially, so they won't have the same number of carers. It's a private one, not officially on the hospital list yet. A friend told me it's being set up by a woman whose teenage daughter ran away from home when she discovered she was pregnant, and then died.'

Callie thanked her for the information and set off for the phone. She could only imagine the feelings of guilt that were driving the poor woman to set up some sort of refuge, but directing Steph to somewhere that could fold before the end of her pregnancy might not be the best course.

Fifteen minutes later she had to admit that she was out of options and started to dial the number written on the bottom of the list in the receptionist's neat script. The sight of the woman's surname startled her for a moment and brought back one of her worst memories from the time she had been doing her rotation in Obs and Gyn.

'Yeah?' said a bored voice when the phone was answered, the sound barely audible over the racket going on in the background.

'Is that The Place to Go?' Callie asked, wondering if she'd misdialled.

'Yeah,' said the same bored voice.

'Is Mrs Keeley there?'

'Who? Oh, you mean *Marian*. Nah. She had to take Jess to 'ospital. 'Er waters broke,' she offered, with the first glimpse of real emotion in her voice.

'Which hospital did they go to?' Callie asked over a superstitious shiver when she heard the woman's first name. What were the chances that there were two people called Marian Keeley who had each lost a pregnant teenage daughter? What were the chances that she would be the one who had provided the spark that had made Callie decide between specialising in Obs and Gyn and A and E?

'She's taken 'er to City. It's where we all go when it's time,' said the laconic voice on the other end of the line. 'Can I take a message? I dunno when she'll be back, mind. Babies can take hours to be born sometimes. And it can hurt a lot, too,' she added with an audible edge of fear to her voice.

'That's why they give you gas and air to breathe,' Callie said matter-of-factly. 'To take the pain away.'

'You've got kids?' she interrupted, almost eagerly.

'No, but I'm a—'

'Well, what would you know about it, then?' the girl snapped, and Callie was left with the dial tone burring in her ear.

'That went well,' she muttered wryly as she replaced the receiver and made her way back towards the curtained cubicles.

'Come with me, Callie,' Steph said as soon as she caught sight of her. 'They're taking me up to the place where they do scans.'

Callie hadn't done anything about finding herself accommodation for the night yet, but she couldn't bring herself to rebuff the youngster, not when she was the closest thing she had to a friend.

She let Steph's nervous chatter wash over her as she rationalised that she could always book into a hotel for one night, even if it meant she had to start looking for a job sooner rather than later. Also, if they were going up to the antenatal department for the ultrasound, it might be close enough to the labour ward for her to see if she could make contact with Marian Keeley.

'Callie! Look!' Steph exclaimed a little while later as she saw the indistinct image appear on the screen. All her fear and disappointment seemed to have been banished by that one shadowy impression with its tiny heart beating so valiantly. 'It's the baby! *My* baby!' she whispered, with a mixture of fear and awe as the being growing inside her became real for the first time. 'Look! It's moving!'

It felt as if a giant vice was being tightened inexorably around Callie's heart. She could remember all too clearly her own terrified joy when she'd seen her baby's heart beating, and for the first time had allowed herself to hope that she and Con would finally have their miracle.

'Would you like a picture to keep?' the technician asked.

The intense look of longing that swept across the youngster's face was a far cry from the resigned defensiveness she'd worn as a shield when Callie had first met her. Her 'Yes! Please,' was every bit as fervent as Callie's had been, and she had no doubt that it would be evidence of a precious memory, as her own early scans had been.

Then, she'd been amazed how different it had been to look at the scan of her own child rather than that of a patient. With professional distance between them, she'd been able to look at the images analytically; when it had been her own baby, she'd demanded, 'Is the baby all right?' every bit as anxiously as any other expectant mother.

'Everything looks fine so far,' the voice interrupted her thoughts. 'No sign that your accident did any damage to the baby or to the placenta.'

'So that means I can go?' Steph said, although Callie thought she could detect a little less eagerness in the words than before. Perhaps the young girl was actually feeling the reassurance of having so much professional help around her.

'Not until the morning,' the midwife who had been assigned to Steph said firmly. 'Although it was brief, you did suffer some loss of consciousness, so we'd like to keep you under observation for a while just as a precaution. In your case, that's more important because of the baby. Anyway,' she added cheerfully, 'it will give you a chance to look us over and get to know us before you come in for the real thing.'

It was another half an hour before Steph was settled in the small four-room ward with two heavily pregnant companions, and Callie was glad to see that both of them were so eager for the novelty of a new person to talk to that they weren't about to let her young friend's defensive prickles put them off.

Callie had almost forgotten about contacting Marian Keeley until she was leaving the antenatal side of the department. She'd turned into the reception area and couldn't help glancing through the safety glass panel in the doors that divided the mothers with babies from those without.

Right at the other end of the corridor she caught sight of a bustle as several people in theatre scrubs were rushing towards the door with the sign for the delivery room hanging above it.

'Jess's baby?' she murmured aloud, and wondered if there was any way she could find out without asking the staff to break patient confidentiality. If the baby had already arrived, she might have missed her chance to meet the woman she hoped would have a suitable place for Steph. If Jess was still in labour, she might still be able to speak to her.

'Can I help you?' said the young midwife, who emerged from the room just the other side of the doors and pushed one of them open to speak to her. 'It's husbands only at the moment.

General visiting hours don't start until seven, after the evening meal is over.'

'It was one of your visitors I was hoping to catch,' Callie said with a smile. 'I'm looking for Marian Keeley. She came in with Jess…'

'Ah, you're one of Marian's new volunteers, are you?' she said with a sudden welcoming smile. 'Come in and have a cup of coffee while you're waiting for her. She shouldn't be long now. Jess is already pushing and…'

At the far end of the corridor there was the sound of a faint wail and her smile grew even wider.

'Oh, I do love that sound!' she exclaimed as she beckoned Callie into the room behind her. 'I've delivered dozens already, but it still gives me a thrill. I'm Jenny, by the way. How do you take your coffee? Milk and sugar? I'll make one for Marian as soon as she's settled Jess onto the ward.'

'I'm Callie,' she offered distractedly, her innate honesty urging her to confess that she wasn't one of Marian's volunteers, but what *could* she say? That she'd never met the woman? That might not be true if she was the same Marian Keeley she'd met nearly two years ago. 'Milk with just the tiniest bit of sugar would be perfect,' she said in the end, deciding that explanations could wait until she came face to face with the refuge's owner.

'Surely you're not watching your weight. You certainly don't need to,' chatted the young woman as she spooned instant coffee into two mugs and waited for the kettle to boil.

'Trying to cut down on my coffee intake by making it less palatable,' Callie admitted wryly. 'At one time I was drinking it black and nearly thick enough to stand a spoon up.' It had been one way of getting through the brutal regime that doctors put themselves through to qualify and she'd virtually become addicted to the stuff. Then she'd heard that it could be a factor for couples experiencing difficulty in conceiving and was definitely frowned on for pregnant mums and had completely cut it out of her diet.

Even though it had been nearly five months since she'd lost her precious baby she hadn't returned to her former coffee intake, feeling as if it would be some sort of admission that she'd given up all hopes of motherhood.

'How do you stand on the subject of biscuits—chocolate biscuits, to be precise?' Jenny asked as she held up a rather posh tin. 'A gift from some very happy parents.'

'Biscuits are definitely one of the major food groups and chocolate is essential for the existence of civilisation,' Callie declared solemnly, then grinned as she beckoned the tin closer.

'Is this a private party or is there room for one more?' said a voice at the door. 'I'm gasping for a cup of tea.'

'Marian!' Jenny said as she leapt to her feet, but Callie hadn't needed the unintentional introduction. The woman in the doorway was someone she'd never forgotten even though she no longer resembled the grief-ridden fury she'd last encountered.

She saw the moment that the bereaved woman recognised her and braced herself for another tirade.

'Dr Lowell!' she gasped and stared at her open-mouthed for several startled seconds before hurrying into the room. To Callie's utter amazement the woman bent to throw her arms around her for a fervent hug. 'Oh, Dr Lowell, I'm so glad to see you. I tried to contact you at the hospital but they said you weren't on Maternity any more and I've felt so guilty...*so* guilty for what I said to you that day... And it *wasn't* your fault...I *knew* it wasn't your fault... That you'd done your best to save Lisa... That it was *my* fault if it was anyone's that she'd gone off like that, and—'

'Hey, Marian, slow down,' said Jenny, clearly stunned by the woman's unexpected reaction to her visitor. 'What's going on here? Callie said she was one of your volunteers.'

'Actually, I didn't...' Callie began, unhappy with the implication that she'd lied, even though she knew she hadn't corrected the midwife's mistaken assumption. Marian's voice overrode hers easily.

'I should be so lucky!' she exclaimed with a dramatic roll of her eyes as she slumped into the nearest chair, clearly well at home in the room. 'Jenny, I don't know whether she's said anything, but this is the doctor I was telling you about a little while ago. She was there when my Lisa died. She and her husband were the ones who saved my granddaughter's life.'

CHAPTER THREE

'I'M SORRY, sir, but there's nothing I can do,' said the policeman in a world-weary tone totally at odds with his youthful appearance. 'From what you've told me, your wife left home of her own accord and—'

'But you don't understand,' Con interrupted, on the verge of screaming with frustration at yet another example of bureaucratic stonewalling. 'She suffered a traumatic loss not many weeks ago. Our baby was stillborn. This is totally uncharacteristic for her. She would never walk out on our marriage or her job like this. *Never.*'

'I'm sorry, sir, but…'

The polite half-smile was so infuriating, making him feel as if the man was patronising him for being concerned. 'Don't you care that something dreadful may have happened to her? That she might even try to commit suicide or—?'

'That would be more in your line, Doctor,' he interrupted flatly. 'Depression isn't a legal matter so much as a medical one. Legally, if your wife decides to walk away, there's absolutely nothing we can do about it other than to list her as a missing person after forty-eight hours.'

Con stabbed his fingers through his hair, tempted to pull it out in handfuls. He knew how fragile Callie was at the moment. He'd been devastated when they'd been told their precious baby's heart wasn't beating any more; he could only imagine how much worse it must have felt to her, knowing that the child she'd sheltered inside her own body had died before it could be born.

He'd been tiptoeing around on eggshells while he'd waited for her to sort things out in her head…waited for her to be ready to come and talk to him about her feelings the way she always had…at least, the way she always had until now.

Being patient had been a struggle for him. It was an intrinsic part of his character that he'd always gone after what he wanted…the way he had when he'd met Callie for the first time. He'd known the moment he'd seen her that he was attracted to her and within minutes of speaking to her had started a determined campaign to persuade her that they were perfect for each other.

And they had been, in spite of everything that life had thrown at them…at least, that was what he'd believed.

Never in his wildest dreams would he have imagined that she would just walk away from him…from their marriage.

'Sir?' prompted the duty constable in a slightly more conciliatory tone. 'Sometimes people feel they just have to go away when they need some time to themselves…time to think. Often they'll get in contact with another member of the family or a friend. It might be worthwhile making a list of your wife's family and close friends and giving them all a call.'

Callie would hate that, Con thought as he trudged wearily out of the police station. She was an intensely private person and if she found out that he'd been telling all and sundry that she'd…what? Blown a fuse? Gone crazy? Well, she really *would* go crazy then.

As for that note she'd left him… Why on earth would he want to divorce the only woman he'd ever loved? The whole idea was completely…crazy.

There was only one person that he could go to and that was Martin Nimmo. Not only had he known the man since they'd been at school together, but his old friend had gone into law and had handled any legal matters that he and Callie had needed from time to time. He had absolutely no intention of following her instructions, but if Callie's depression had her confused enough to think of such a thing, then at some stage she would be getting in contact with Martin.

'Hi, Martin, it's Callie,' she said, her heart a lead weight in her chest as she contemplated the irrevocable step she was taking. Would Con have already been in contact with his old friend to set things in motion?

'Hey, beautiful!' he exclaimed. 'I haven't heard from the two of you in ages. I hope you're ringing to invite me for another of your delicious home-cooked meals.'

'N-not exactly,' she stammered, surprised just how hard one simple phone call could be. 'I—I wondered if Con has been in contact with you yet?'

'No… As I said, I haven't heard from either of you in…' He stopped suddenly. 'Callie? What's the matter? You sound strange. Has something happened? Is Con all right? Are you?'

'W-we're all right…sort of,' she said with a hitch in her voice as tears threatened. Martin was one of the few people who knew just how long the two of them had been trying to start their family. 'I—I mean, we haven't had any accidents or anything. It's just… Con'll be contacting you soon to do whatever you need to do to sort out about the divorce.'

'Divorce?' he echoed in disbelief, then burst out laughing. 'Oh, very funny, Callie. You had me going there for a minute. If there's any couple *not* likely to divorce it's you and Con. So, why *did* you ring? Is it that invitation for a poor bachelor otherwise condemned to a diet of junk food?'

'Martin, I'm not joking,' Callie said as the tears started slipping down her cheeks. 'I've moved out of the house… moved away completely so I won't be an embarrassment to him when he—'

'Callie, what the hell's going on?' he interrupted sharply, no laughter in his voice now. 'You're crazy about the guy and he loves you, too. What—?'

'Not any m-more,' she hiccuped, fighting the gathering flood of tears. 'I just wanted to let you know that I'll be in touch again as soon as I'm settled somewhere, so you'll know where to send the papers.'

'Damn the papers!' he snapped, clearly rattled. 'Callie, talk to me. Tell me what's been going on. Something must have been, to get the two of you in such a state. And it must all be a monumental misunderstanding because there's no way—'

'I'm sorry, Martin, but I—I just can't…can't talk about it,' she interrupted, hating to be rude to someone who had been a good friend to both of them, but this was so much harder than she'd thought it would be. 'Speak to Con. He'll tell you all about it.'

This had definitely not been one of her better ideas, she realised as she tried to mop up her tears without letting Martin know she was crying or attracting too much attention from the people around her.

She'd been waiting for Marian to say her farewells to Jess and the new baby before she drove Callie to see her new venture, and she'd decided to make use of the time by contacting Martin. She obviously should have waited until she was somewhere more private than a telephone kiosk that was little more than a clear plastic bubble.

'I—I'll call you in a little while,' she promised before she fumbled the receiver into its cradle and sobbed.

A persistent tapping beside her head had her hastily smearing the tears away with both hands before she turned to face the elderly gentleman standing nearby.

'Are you all right, missy?' he asked in concerned tones. 'Is there anything I can do?'

'There's nothing anyone can do,' she said bleakly before she could put a curb on her tongue. 'I'm sorry. That was rude,' she apologised swiftly when he blinked at the rebuff. 'I'm all right, really. I just…had some bad news and…'

'Take yourself home and make yourself a cup of tea,' he advised kindly, giving her arm a pat with a gnarled, blue-veined hand. 'I find that even if it doesn't make the problem go away, it sometimes makes it easier to cope with.'

'The magic properties of tea,' she said with a watery smile just as Marian approached.

'Ready to go?' she asked cheerfully, pausing long enough for Callie to say goodbye to the gallant gentleman. 'There's going to be pandemonium when I tell the rest of the girls about Jess's baby. They're going to want to celebrate, big time, so we'll have to stop off to get some pizza and rent a couple of videos.'

The thought of an evening spent eating pizza and watching a film sounded so simple and normal that Callie felt like crying again.

Sometimes over the last few weeks it had felt as if nothing would ever be normal again.

'Are you sure I won't be intruding? Wouldn't you rather drop me off at the nearest B and B? If I come in the morning you can show me round,' she offered.

'You're not going to escape that easily,' Marian teased. 'I don't know why you've moved to this area, but if there's the slightest chance that I can persuade you to give up a few hours to help us out, I'm going to grab it with both hands.'

'The hospital receptionist mentioned that you were having problems with funding and getting volunteers,' Callie said. 'How long have you been open?'

'Officially, we're not open yet,' Marian said wryly. 'There is an absolute mountain of paperwork to climb if you want to set up any sort of refuge that will be eligible for public funding, and the house was in a terrible state when I took it on.' She shrugged. 'It was the only way I could afford to get something big enough to do what I wanted and I'm having to do most of the work myself if I can't twist people's arms to help me.'

'So, if you're not open yet…?'

'Jess was the first one I took in because she just didn't have anywhere else to go. She collapsed in front of me in the post office,' she said as she led the way to her slightly battered-looking car. 'There had been some problem with a money order being delayed and she hadn't eaten for three days, so I took her to the hospital to make certain she was all right then brought her home with me when she was released and she's been—' The sharp intrusion of a mobile phone stopped her recounting the tale before she'd even got as far as putting the key in the ignition.

'Marian Keeley at The Place to Go,' she said into the neat little instrument, and Callie knew that the fact that she was smiling would be heard on the other end of the line.

'Can you speak up, sweetheart? I can't hear you very well,' she said after a moment. 'Can you tell me your name?'

There was a pause while Marian concentrated fiercely on whatever her caller was saying, her free hand covering her other ear to help her to hear.

'Jodie? Listen to me,' Marian interrupted, and although it didn't show in her voice Callie could see that something she'd heard had made her companion furiously angry, her grey eyes shooting sparks. 'Tell me where you are, sweetheart, and I'll come and find you. I'll come straight away, I promise.'

There were several more seconds of silence before she broke in again. 'I know exactly where you mean and I'm on my way, Jodie,' she said. 'When I get to the shopping arcade I'll pull up by the kerb and switch my headlights on and off. The back doors will be unlocked. I'm only five minutes away, sweetheart. Hang on.'

By the time she flipped the phone closed to break the connection and turned to explain, Callie was waiting with her seat belt fastened.

'Go!' she said. 'Tell me what it's about while you're driving.'

'Are you sure?' Marian said with a frown. 'This sounds as if it could get a bit…hairy.'

'And you think I haven't seen hairy while working in A and E?' Callie scoffed. 'The latest figures claimed that one in three of the staff has been physically assaulted on duty. Get going and tell me what's happened to Jodie.'

'Unfortunately, it's more of the same... underage and pregnant but this time with battery thrown in,' the older woman said grimly as she accelerated through a junction just before the lights changed. 'She thought her boyfriend would be as pleased about the baby as she was but...to quote her...he freaked and beat her up to try to make her miscarry.'

Callie grimaced. She'd seen the results of something similar not long ago. 'She must be terrified. I take it that she's hiding from him?' Callie asked as they approached the end of the town that was largely deserted now that most of the shops were closed for the day. The trendy bars and clubs that usually provided the night life in such cities must be situated somewhere else.

'How did you guess?' Marian said wryly as she slowed the car, her eyes sweeping from side to side. 'She's probably been ducking from one shadow to the next.' She finally drew up at the side of the road near the entrance to the pedestrians-only shopping precinct and, as she'd described, switched her headlights off and on again.

'I can't see anyone,' Callie whispered, her eyes now trying to probe every dark corner, too, looking for a sign of movement.

'Well, I know I'm in the right place because she said she'd make for this entrance…between the parade of shops,' Marian said with a deepening frown. 'This row doesn't have those pull-down shutters so she was going to hide in a doorway.'

'Do you think he found her before she was able to make it here? I can't even see a stray cat moving,' Callie murmured as she started her systematic inspection again. 'There's just a bundle of rags someone's left in the corner over there and… Oh, Marian! I think that's her! She's collapsed…'

Even as she spoke she was frantically stabbing at the button to release her seat belt while her other hand was reaching for the doorhandle.

The car surged forward the extra few yards as she swung her door open so that she was just the width of the pavement away from the pathetic little heap of humanity when her feet hit the ground.

'Jodie?' she said gently as she touched the slender shoulder and felt the tremors that shook her. 'Can you hear me?'

'I hurt,' she moaned. 'Help me…'

Somewhere behind her she heard an angry shout and felt Jodie shudder in reaction. Had the man who had done this to her found them? Was he going to try to stop them taking her for help? There was no time to do any sort of survey of her injuries. She was just going to have to get her into the car as best she could and hope that she didn't do her any further damage.

'I've got to get you up on your feet, Jodie. We need to get you into the car. Tell me if I hurt you anywhere,' she said as she scooped one arm underneath the girl's slender body and wrapped the other one around her. 'Help me, Jodie,' she pleaded, knowing she wouldn't be able to lift her and carry her even such a short distance in time to get her away from the approaching thud of running feet.

'Good girl,' she praised when the shivering child found a surge of strength to help Callie to get her upright.

'Hey! You!' bellowed a voice that was approaching far too fast for comfort. 'Leave her alone!'

'No chance,' Callie muttered through gritted teeth as she staggered sideways for several paces then pivoted to throw herself backwards through the door that Marian had swung open and drag Jodie into the back of the car with her. 'Pull your feet in, Jodie. Quick!' she ordered as she continued to shuffle backwards across the seat with her elbows and heels until she hit the opposite door. 'Go, Marian. Go!'

Marian took off like a scalded cat, the acceleration she forced out of the ancient car enough to slam the door shut just as their pursuer was reaching into the car to grab one of Jodie's ankles.

There was a dreadful howl as they left him behind that seemed to echo around the interior of the car until they'd almost reached the hospital.

'Ignore any signs for car parking, Marian. Head straight to the accident and emergency department,' Callie directed as they turned through the brightly lit entrance to the hospital grounds, all the while her fingers busily charting her fragile patient's pulse and respiration as best she could in the limited light of the car's interior. She didn't like what she found but couldn't say anything for fear of frightening Jodie about the seriousness of her condition. 'If you can see the ambulance bay for emergency admissions, aim for that. If it's anything like my hospital, it'll be a shortcut through the triage procedure straight to a doctor.'

Marian must have picked up something in her voice because she hooted repeatedly as she flew into a space, applied her brakes and flung her door open right next to an ambulance that looked as if it had only recently arrived.

'Help! We need help here!' she shouted as she scrambled out of the driver's seat. Callie nearly fell out of the car backwards when the door was opened behind her, but a strong pair of hands was there to catch her.

'What have you brought us, love?' said a reassuring male voice.

'This is Jodie,' Callie said as the ambulance-man helped her to slide carefully out from under her slumped burden. It was important that she pass on every scrap of the information she'd managed to get out of the badly injured child. 'She's fourteen, pregnant and she's been beaten up. Her breathing is spontaneous but ragged. Her pulse was initially around eighty but it's now over a hundred and climbing. She has tenderness and guarding over the epigastric region and it's becoming increasingly rigid,' she added as she stood aside to allow the man to assess the best way of getting Jodie out. 'She's definitely losing blood somewhere. Spleen perhaps? She needs IV fluids and the fastest possible track to surgery,'

There was an exclamation from the other side of the car where his colleague had opened the other door by Jodie's feet.

'Eew! I've just found some amputated digits trapped in the door. Do they belong to any of you?'

Callie's gorge rose when she realised the significance of the howl she'd heard when they'd driven away. 'They belong to whoever did this to Jodie,' she said grimly. 'He might turn up looking for attention for his injuries.'

'We'll warn Security to look out for him,' said the man with the paramedic's flash on his uniform as he dropped them into a plastic bag then pushed them unceremoniously into a pocket.

Between them it only took moments to lift Jodie out of the car and onto the trolley that Marian had commandeered, but when Callie would have stepped back to allow them to hurry their patient inside, Jodie reached out and grabbed her sleeve.

'Please,' she whispered with a feverish expression in her eyes. 'I don't want to lose my baby. It's all I've got.'

'Everyone will do their best, Jodie,' Callie promised as she kept pace with the rapidly moving trolley to maintain her hold on the young girl's hand. Her heart nearly broke when she saw the childish fingers with the chewed fingernails and chipped polish. 'Just trust them and concentrate on getting better.'

She didn't know whether Jodie had even heard what she'd said because the youngster had finally lost her hold on consciousness, and all Callie could think was that she wished it was *Con's* hands she was entrusting with the child's welfare. The two of them, working together, were a formidable team that…

'I'm Dr Ferenghi,' said a softly accented voice behind Callie and she and Marian turned to find a tiny little doll of a woman wearing an outsize white coat with a stethoscope draped around her neck. 'I've phoned up to warn Theatre that the patient will be on her way at any moment, but it would be helpful to have a few more details about her.'

'We know very little more than you do,' Marian said grimly, her face pale as she watched blood being drawn for cross-matching and IVs being inserted while another member of staff was swiftly attaching monitoring equipment. It was obvious to Callie that the poor woman was reliving those awful frantic last moments of her own daughter's life. Callie almost took over the telling for her but then realised that it would help her to cope with the memories better if she had something else to focus on. 'She's pregnant, she's been beaten up by the father of the child and she phoned me for help.'

'And you are...her mother?' the young doctor said with a puzzled frown, only a small part of her concentration on the conversation, the major part tracking everything that was going on around Jodie. She might look no older than the patient herself but from the little she said to the other members of the team, it was obvious that she knew exactly what she was doing.

'No. I'm Marian Keeley and I'm trying to set up a refuge for girls like Jodie.'

'Ah! The Place to Go!' she exclaimed as a wide smile beamed out at them. 'We have heard of you already in A and E. God bless you for what you are trying to do for these girls. Now, it is time for Jodie to go up to Theatre,' she announced as the frantic choreography around the unconscious figure came to a climax and the trolley was pushed rapidly along the corridor away from them, with every monitor shrilling out a warning.

* * *

Callie's eyes flicked up to check the kitchen clock again, frustrated that they hadn't heard anything yet. Surely Jodie couldn't still be in Theatre? Had someone simply forgotten to notify them of her condition because neither she nor Marian was related to the girl?

'The waiting can drive you mad, can't it?' Marian said as she brought a freshly made pot of tea to the table to join the mugs and jug of milk she'd already collected.

'This is worse than usual for me because it's not my own hospital,' Callie admitted. 'At least there I could just pick up a phone and ask for an update. Here…' She shrugged. 'It's just been so long since she went in…'

'Why do you think I brought you back here?' Marian asked wryly. 'I knew that showing you around the place and introducing you to my girls would keep your mind off Jodie for a while, but you still haven't told me what you think of it.'

'I think it's brilliant,' Callie declared honestly. 'It's not institutional in the least, far more like a real home, with the girls choosing the colours for their rooms and helping to do the painting.'

'Strictly non-toxic paints, of course,' Marian interjected. 'But the DIY is largely a case of need rather than choice. I just haven't got the money to pay anyone to do the cosmetic stuff. It cost enough to get the basic building renovations done and as for putting in the extra bathrooms…'

'So, where did the name come from?' Callie asked as she took her first sip of the steaming brew. 'Why did you call it The Place to Go?'

'I was playing around with a design for some flyers and posters…for when I'm finally official…and I was jotting down ideas like *Nowhere to go?* or *Need a place to stay?* and ended up with *The Place to Go*. Anyway, so many people have been referring to it as that in all the weeks and months that I've been going the rounds of the bureaucrats that it's just stuck.'

'Well, it's obviously memorable enough so that people like Jodie knew she could ring you for help,' Callie commented.

'Thank goodness,' Marian said fervently. 'If

only there'd been something similar when Lisa needed it, especially when she felt that she couldn't come to me...' She bit her lips, clearly still badly affected by the senseless death of her daughter.

'I don't know if it's any help, Marian, but Lisa was able to talk to me for a few moments,' Callie offered, those few brief sentences imprinted on her memory by the other circumstances surrounding them.

'Lisa spoke to you?' Marian gasped. 'But I thought... I was told that you and your husband were the ones who did the surgery, and she would have been unconscious for that.'

'We did, but we had to wait a couple of minutes for the anaesthetist to get everything organised to put her under before we could start and... Marian, I feel so guilty because Lisa gave me a message for you and I've never been able to deliver it.' The poor woman had been so distraught at her daughter's death that she hadn't been in any fit state to listen, hitting out verbally at the first person to come near her.

'A message for *me*?' she whispered in disbelief. 'Lisa spoke about me…after all the rows we'd had and the fact I hadn't seen her for months, and…?'

'I think she had a premonition,' Callie said as she reached out to touch the white-knuckled hands clenched on the table. 'Her blood pressure had shot up sky high, she had protein in her urine and all her systems were in chaos and shutting down, but she was totally calm when she said, "Tell my mum I love her and I'm sorry I was such a disappointment to her. Tell her that I hope my baby's a girl so she'll have a second chance." But then she started convulsing and by the time we operated to get the baby out, it was already too late for Lisa. The eclampsia was so severe that she'd gone into multi-organ failure and her brain had been so badly damaged that—'

'I *know* that there wasn't anything more you could have done for Lisa,' Marian interrupted with emotional tears in her eyes. 'I think I knew it right from the start, and I'm so sorry I turned on you that way, but…I was just so shocked that she'd died from something as ordinary and everyday as pregnancy.'

'Perhaps it's because we've become so accustomed to all the high-tech diagnostic equipment around these days,' Callie suggested. 'Sometimes we forget that women have always died carrying children and giving birth to them, no matter how good the health care system surrounding them. The percentages may have gone down, but it is still one of the most dangerous things we women can put ourselves through.' To say nothing of the multiplication of dangers that happened with repeated courses of IVF, she added to herself. And to go through all of that and end up with no baby...

'I found out afterwards that Lisa hadn't had any antenatal care at all,' Marian told her. 'I suppose she was so young that she still believed that refusing to think about something would make it go away. If you hadn't been so quick off the mark...'

'Not quick enough to save Lisa,' Callie pointed out, still feeling guilty that she hadn't been able to save the youngster.

'But quick enough to give Emmylou a fighting chance,' Marian countered as she reached out for a photo tucked on the cluttered work surface nearby and passed it to Callie. 'This is my grand-daughter, Emma Louise, on the day she was born. Lisa chose her daughter's name when she was about four years old and never changed her mind.'

Again, Callie caught the glitter of tears in her eyes as she smiled at the image of the same tiny scrap in the incubator that Callie had last seen the day she'd left the department for the final time, the day she'd decided that Obs and Gyn wasn't the career for her, not if she wanted to keep her sanity.

'When she went into the intensive care unit they said her chances of survival were less than fifty per cent,' Marian continued. 'She was so premature and underweight because Lisa's diet had been so poor and...' She shook her head. 'Every time I left the unit to go home, I expected to be called back to be told she'd died.'

'And?' Emma Louise had only been a few weeks less premature than her own tiny baby. How many days or weeks had she managed to struggle before she'd given up the unequal battle? Her own precious child hadn't even drawn his first breath.

'And you'll meet her in the morning, I hope, but in the meantime this was taken on her first birthday.' Marian held out another photo, this one of a bright, laughing toddler sitting in a high chair with chocolate cake smeared all over her chubby cheeks.

'She *lived*?' Callie gasped in disbelief, gazing wide-eyed at the evidence. The baby she'd last seen had been so fragile that she'd barely managed to draw her next breath, even with assistance. This child looked as if she'd never had a day's illness in her life.

'She not only lived, but she survived without any apparent deficiencies from her early arrival. She's absolutely perfect,' Marian said enthusiastically, every inch the doting grandmother. 'She's nearly two now, bright as a button and was endlessly patient when the girls used her for live practice of feeding, bathing and nappy changing. They certainly knew how to cope with a wriggly baby by the time their own came along.'

Callie forced herself to hand the photo back, reluctant to let go of such an enchanting image.

'So,' Marian said as she stood the photo frame back on the side, 'I don't know what brought you up to this part of the country, but what I need to know is how can I get you to volunteer some time at The Place?'

'Volunteer?' Half of Callie's brain was still focused on the little she could see of that perfect baby smile, so it took her a moment to work out what Marian was talking about and several more to realise the significance of it.

'I'm not in a position to pay anyone a regular wage unless or until we get some funding from somewhere,' Marian explained apologetically. 'That's why I've been having to do almost everything single-handed. Eventually, I'm hoping to have some qualified staff on call in case we have any problems, a counsellor or a nurse perhaps, but…'

'What about resident staff?' Callie suggested. 'Obviously, in the normal run of things you wouldn't want or need a doctor on the premises as most of your girls' problems centre around their homelessness rather than serious health concerns. But if one were available and willing…'

Marian was quick on the uptake. 'You're suggesting that you would be willing to move in here, that you'd act as resident medical assistance?' She looked as if she didn't know whether delight or dismay was going to win the battle inside her. 'But I've just told you that I can't afford to pay you a salary…certainly nothing like you can earn at the hospital.'

'And if I were willing, in the short term, to provide my services in exchange for a roof over my head and a place at the table at mealtimes?' Callie suggested, surreptitiously crossing her fingers. She didn't know why she hadn't realised earlier that this would be an ideal solution to her immediate problem of finding an affordable place to stay. It would give her some much-needed breathing space to sort out what she wanted to do with the rest of her life while providing the help that Marian so badly needed.

'Then I would apologise for the fact that your new room hasn't been decorated yet, but promise to help you do the scrubbing and painting by way of saying welcome,' Marian said with the suspicious gleam of tears in her eyes.

'What a day…!' Callie whispered as she slid wearily between sheets worn thin through repeated washing. Neither she nor Marian had been able to go to bed until they'd found out how Jodie had fared. It had been a relief to hear that she'd survived the splenectomy but dreadful to learn that she'd lost so much blood from her injuries that she'd arrested on the table.

Marian hadn't understood the significance of the fact that Jodie had needed shocking to persuade her heart to beat normally again. It had only been when Callie had explained that the surge of electricity necessary would have killed the baby that she'd understood Callie's distress. It was going to be difficult for Jodie to learn that the baby she'd wanted so desperately to protect had died to save her own life.

At least the news about Steph had been better, with no signs of concussion and a normal scan to reassure her.

With Jess and her new baby staying in the maternity unit for a few days, Marian had suggested that Steph could join them at The Place to Go, if she wanted to, so the problem of finding her a safe place to stay had been solved, too.

'It'll mean we all have to pitch in and get another room finished before Jess comes home,' Marian warned. 'At the moment, the girls are sharing, two to a room, but I want the new mums to come home to a room of their own that they will share with their baby. I'm convinced that it will help to reinforce the fact that they are now totally responsible for that tiny life.'

'Rather than the girl's life continuing almost as before, with the baby as a completely separate entity banished to a distant nursery?' Callie commented, seeing the basic sense in the theory. 'But at the same time, with you and the other girls around to lend a hand when they're struggling, they won't feel nearly so overwhelmed as if they were trying to cope on their own in those first few weeks.'

'So, are you up for a bit of paper-stripping

and sandpapering in the morning?' Marian challenged.

'Not if I don't get some sleep,' Callie groaned. The day had been physically tiring, with the long journey, but it was primarily the emotional devastation of the last few weeks that had left her so completely exhausted.

Her new room had definitely seen better days but at least the damage was mostly cosmetic. If only her own damage were that superficial.

Con's laughing face appeared behind her closed eyelids and her heart clenched in agony.

He had been the one constant in her life since the day she'd met him, endlessly loving and supporting through the end of their gruelling training and the early, inexplicably childless years of their marriage. He'd seemed totally committed, too, to their repeated clinical attempts to have the family they wanted, but did she really know what he'd been thinking and feeling? Or had the stillbirth of their tiny son simply been the final straw?

Part of her wanted desperately to know what had gone so wrong between them, but it would be embarrassing for both of them if she were to break down in front of him, begging and pleading for another chance—pointless, too, when he'd already moved on in his heart.

'Oh, Con, I miss you…' she whispered into the night.

CHAPTER FOUR

'HERE, Con, I made you a coffee…no sugar and a splash of milk, right?' said an all-too-familiar voice as soon as he stepped inside the staff lounge. 'I heard you say you were going to take a break and it coincided with mine.'

Con only just stopped himself groaning aloud. Sonja Heggarty…again. Did the woman do *any* work? It seemed as if every time he turned around she was there in front of him with that wide white smile, the impossibly blonde hair and her…assets prominently on display.

'Sorry. I don't have time for a coffee,' he said bluntly. He really didn't have the energy or inclination to be polite this morning. He was so worried about Callie that he'd barely closed his eyes all night. 'I've got some phone calls to make,' he said, as he swiftly retrieved the mobile phone he'd forgotten in his locker and strode past her and out of the room without a sideways glance.

In less than a minute he was outside, the chilly wind cutting through the scant protection of a white coat thrown over a set of cotton scrubs as he rounded the corner of the building housing the A and E department. He switched the phone on as he was walking and it rang immediately, as though someone had been waiting impatiently for that moment.

'Callie, where *are* you?' he demanded, without glancing at the caller display, his need to know that she was safe making him certain that she must be his caller.

'It's not Callie, it's me,' said his old friend's voice sharply. 'Con, what the hell have you been up to? What have you done to Callie?'

'I don't know… Nothing!' he exclaimed defensively, then realised that Martin's call had to mean that Callie had been in touch with him. 'Martin, when did you speak to her? Where is she? Is she all right?'

'You mean, apart from the fact that she could hardly string two words together because she was trying not to cry?' Martin blasted him. 'What have you been doing to hurt her so much? Playing away from home with some bimbo nurse with yo-yo knickers?'

'No!' Con snapped, revulsion surging through him at the very thought. From the day he'd met her, Callie had been the only woman with whom he wanted to share the ultimate intimacy of making love.

'Then why did she phone me to tell me that you would be getting in contact to start divorce proceedings?' Martin charged harshly. 'Even a two-time loser like me can recognise that Callie thinks you hung the moon and stars, so I know *she* hasn't done anything to—'

'Martin, I *haven't*. I *wouldn't*,' Con interrupted heatedly. 'I've absolutely no idea what's going on. I went home yesterday morning after the end of my shift to find she'd disappeared…just left me a note. Man, if you know where she is, you've *got* to tell me so I can go to her. We need to talk to work this all out. She needs to come home.'

'I can't tell you where she is because I don't

know,' Martin said shortly, and when Con heard the lingering suspicion in his voice he was shocked to realise that he wasn't sure that his friend had believed him.

'Well, where was she phoning from?' Con demanded squashing the feeling down. At the moment, whether his friend believed that he'd kept his wedding vows or not was the least of his worries. 'Do you know *that* much?' If necessary, he'd take time off from work and drive around until he found her, but he needed to know which area to search.

'All I can tell you is that she phoned from a call box,' Martin said grudgingly. 'I could hear some sort of public announcement in the background, but whether it was at a railway station or an airport, I don't know.'

'Airport?' Con echoed, feeling sick. He hadn't even thought to check whether her passport was missing and there was no way he could walk out on his shift to go and check now.

'So, what do you want me to do?' Martin asked, his tone still rather abrupt. 'I can't act for both of you or there'd be a conflict of interest.

Anyway, I'll need to sit down with Callie and go through all the legalities before I can file divorce papers. You'll both need to decide what you're going to do about the house and—'

'Don't bother,' Con snapped, hurt all over again by the sudden realisation that his oldest friend would choose to represent his wife, instead of him. 'There isn't going to be any divorce, not if I have any say in the matter and certainly not before I've had a face-to-face meeting with Callie to find out why she's taken off like this.'

He scrubbed his free hand over his face, wondering when he was ever going to get a good night's sleep again. It had been months already as he'd lain in the darkness beside Callie, listening to her toss and turn. He'd tried to comfort her in the days after she'd come out of hospital but she'd still been totally overwhelmed by the disaster and while she had often gravitated towards him in the brief hours when she'd slept, the rest of the time she had pushed him away, physically and mentally. Only once had she turned to him and welcomed his caresses, but he'd known she hadn't really been ready for such intimacy when he'd seen the tears on her cheeks and had woken later in the night to hear her stifling her tears in her pillow.

'So, what do you want me to tell her the next time she phones?' his friend prompted, his anger apparently mollified somewhat by Con's vehemence.

'That I need to speak to her. That I need to know where she is, that she's all right…. Oh, Martin, you saw what sort of a state she was in each time the IVF failed. You remember how it got worse every time. Then she was pregnant at last and everything was going well and she was just…so happy she was almost incandescent with it. When they told her the baby had died…' He swallowed hard, unable to continue for a moment.

'You don't think she'd…harm herself, do you?' Martin demanded with horror in his voice. 'She was very *down* the last time I saw her, but…'

'No!' Con denied hotly in an automatic knee-jerk reaction, but then wondered exactly how certain he was. He'd never imagined that Callie would leave him, either.

But, then, she had been so quiet the last day or two—even more withdrawn than before, as though she had been getting worse rather than better. Was that why she'd left? So that she could—?

His pager dragged him unceremoniously out of his nightmare thoughts.

'Martin, I've got to go. I'm still on duty,' he said as he turned to stride back towards the main entrance to A and E. 'But, please...' His throat closed up so tight that he was unable to continue. All he knew was that there was a gaping hole in his chest where his heart used to be, and until Callie was back again...

'If she calls, I'll tell her you want to know where she is and when the two of you can meet up to talk,' his friend finished for him.

'I'll talk to you later,' Con managed as the automatic doors slid open for him, and he flipped the phone shut and dropped it into his pocket as he made for the urgently beckoning figure of Selina.

'I thought I'd lost you,' the A and E manager scolded. 'There's a patient on his way in—a possible heart attack. I've already sent Sonja in to make sure that everything's prepared.'

Con hoped he'd hidden his grimace before it became visible, remembering how short he'd been with the nurse when she'd taken the trouble to make him a coffee. He hoped she wasn't the sort of person to sulk or their time working together to help their patient could be rather uncomfortable. It was going to be hard enough concentrating on treating the possible heart attack while Callie was so much on his mind. The last thing he needed was a pouting nurse to add to the strain.

'Did you manage to finish your phone calls before Selina found you?' Sonja asked brightly, and he wondered vaguely if she realised that bending forward like that made it look as if her…assets were going to spill out of the V neck of her scrub top.

Callie never looked as if she was revealing too much, even when she'd been pregnant and her breasts had grown several bra sizes larger. She'd actually been quite proud of them and he'd enjoyed the novelty of…

'This is Gary Williams,' the paramedic was saying as soon as the trolley pushed its way through the doors, reeling the information off the clipboard in his hand. 'He's a fifty-four-year-old man with no previous history of heart or circulatory problems. Sudden onset of pain in his chest, radiating up the neck into the side of his face and down his left arm.'

Con was automatically taking in the reported details but his hands were already following the familiar path as he performed his own examination. The stark terror in the man's eyes as he grunted with the pain and his clammy grey-tinged skin were enough to tell him there was a serious problem, without the monitors and their tell-tale readouts of falling oxygen perfusion and irregular pulse.

As soon as the leads were in position for the ECG he turned to look at the trace and nearly collided with Staff Nurse Heggarty.

'Excuse me, Staff,' he muttered distractedly, but when he went to step aside he was startled to feel her press her ample curves against his arm.

'Sonja,' she corrected him, and the glance she sent him from under half-lowered lids was obviously meant to be flirtatious.

'For heaven's sake!' he hissed in exasperation, and glared at her as he sidestepped to break the contact. This was neither the time nor the place to practise her feminine wiles, even if he *had* been interested. 'Get on the phone to Geoff Bridgeman, please. We need an urgent cardio consult.' If he didn't miss his guess, their patient was going to need surgery to sort his problem out—probably coronary artery bypass before his heart was damaged beyond repair. In the meantime, all he could do was use every means at his disposal to minimise the damage with clot-busting drugs, pain control and support for his circulation.

If only the pain in his own heart was as simple to ease.

Con was still thinking about Gary Williams, already under the knife for a triple bypass, as he strode swiftly towards the staff lounge. This was another day when he'd missed his meal break, but even though his stomach was growling for food, he couldn't muster up any enthusiasm for eating. All he could think about, when he wasn't frantically busy, was Callie—wondering where she was, what she was doing, whether she was safe, but most of all needing to know why she'd decided to disappear without a single word of warning.

'She's left him, you know,' said a horribly familiar voice as he began to push the door open, and he froze in disbelief. The speaker *couldn't* be talking about Callie, could she? As far as he knew, no one other than Martin and the disinterested policeman he'd spoken to knew about it.

'Well, it stands to reason, doesn't it?' the voice continued. 'A man like him should have a family and she can't…'

'Who told you that?' demanded another voice. 'I heard Callie was taking some sick leave…'

'Well, they *would* say that, wouldn't they?' said the first voice smugly, now unmistakably Sonja Heggarty. 'So much less chance of people gossiping. But I've got a friend in Human Resources and he told me that she's handed in her resignation, effective immediately.'

Con took his hand off the door and let it close gently, shutting that awful gossip away.

He felt sick that the whole hospital apparently knew more than he did.

Had Callie handed in her resignation? Why hadn't anyone mentioned it to him? Did this mean that she wasn't going to come back to St Mark's...ever?

The thought brought him out in a cold sweat. It had been bad enough trying to get through each minute while he was expecting to hear from her at any moment...as soon as she'd sorted her head out. But if he thought he might never see her again...

His heart clenched in his chest and the pain was so sharp that once again he found himself empathising with Gary Williams.

Well, one thing was certain, he thought as he strode away. He wasn't going in there until the gossips had dispersed. It was hard enough coping with Callie's disappearance without knowing that the whole hospital was talking about it.

For a moment despair swamped him and he had to stop and lean his shoulder against the wall.

'Callie,' he whispered softly while his eyes burned with the need to cry. 'Where are you, my love?'

Jodie wasn't fit to come out of hospital for nearly a week after her surgery but the staff on her ward were glad to see her go.

'It's just so hard for the kid,' one of the midwives said when Callie came to collect her. 'There was no bed free to move her into a general surgical ward, so she's been stuck in here with the mums on supervised bed rest.'

'Not the best way to start getting over the loss of her own baby,' Callie agreed with a grimace, having made exactly that point to the senior member of staff on duty each time she'd visited the youngster. Guilt made her wonder if the situation might have been different if she'd mentioned her own expertise in the field, but she didn't want to start any gossip. The less people knew about her, the more chance there was that she might be able to cope with the loss of the life she'd known. 'Has she said much to anyone about what happened to her?'

'Not a single word, as far as the staff knows,' the midwife said with a concerned frown. 'If the circumstances weren't in her file, none of us on the ward would have known. She just seems to be bottling it all up during the day and then sobbing herself to sleep every night. And she's not eating properly, either.'

'Well, we'll have to see if Marian can work her magic,' Callie said, holding up crossed fingers. 'Is she ready for signing out?'

'She's been sitting on her bed with her bag packed for nearly an hour, with those wretched earphones in so she can't hear anyone speak over the music in her ears.'

'Are there any special instructions we need to know?'

'Nothing that you don't know as well as I do—no lifting until the incision's properly healed and finish the course of antibiotics. She's got the prescription in her bag.' She paused, then continued on a different tack. 'So, are we likely to be seeing you again? Marian said you've volunteered as slave labour for a while at that refuge place of hers.'

'I had some time on my hands,' Callie said casually. 'And I'm enjoying doing the decorating. There's something very satisfying about standing in the doorway at the end of a long day and being able to see exactly what you've achieved.'

'Well, rather you than me,' she said, and pulled a face. 'I hate decorating my own place so there's no way I'd volunteer to do someone else's.'

'Speaking of which, it's time I took Jodie to the room we've been preparing for her. The other girls all helped out and will be making curtains and so on later, if they weren't able to do the heavier work.'

'Aren't you going to be putting her in the same situation as we've had here?' the midwife said suddenly. 'Jodie's going to be surrounded by pregnancy and babies at Marian's, too.'

'It *is* a problem, we know, but we haven't really got any option other than leaving her on the streets to sleep rough…and that's no option at all.' It was a situation that Callie had thought about as she'd lain sleepless night after night. At least Jodie didn't have to worry about her attacker finding her. The police had picked Billy up when they'd been tipped off that he'd arrived at the accident department for attention to his damaged hand.

Losing her baby was something completely different. Callie knew only too well how hard it was to see other people waiting for their babies to arrive, knowing that she would never hold her own. All she could hope was that Jodie would let her get close enough to tell her that she understood what the youngster was going through. Perhaps the fact that she'd suffered a similar loss would create a link between them that would let Jodie allow Callie to help her…maybe even form a new connection with her family.

'Where's Marian?' Jodie demanded when Callie tapped her arm and gestured towards her ears. At least the youngster took the hint to remove the headphones, although the tinny driving beat still filled the space between them. Didn't she realise the damage she was doing to her hearing by having it turned up so loud? Still, that was a battle for another day. First, she had to persuade the girl to come with her.

'Marian's waiting for you at home,' Callie said brightly. 'She's supervising the other girls while they finish a little project. They're hoping to get it finished by the time we get there.'

'What's it got to do with me?' Jodie said sullenly. 'You're only taking me there because I've got nowhere else to go.'

'Partly,' Callie agreed as she reached for the plastic bag containing Jodie's pitiful collection of belongings. Most of them had been supplied by Marian when she'd discovered that Jodie had left her boyfriend without taking so much as a toothbrush with her. 'And partly because she's a person who likes to keep her promises.'

'What promises? She didn't make any to me,' she objected even as she allowed herself to be guided into the obligatory waiting wheelchair.

'Not promises to you, personally,' Callie agreed as she set off along the corridor. 'But it's a promise that she's determined The Place to Go keeps to…that they'll find a bed and a hot meal for any girl in trouble. It might not be anything fancy, but you just have to ring up…the way you did the other night…and she'll come and pick you up.'

Jodie was silent until they reached the designated pick-up point near the hospital entrance and she caught sight of Marian's car.

'Is *this* what she was driving that night?' the youngster demanded in disbelief. 'I didn't think it was such a rust-bucket.'

'It's the only car she's got, so, yes, this is the one. It doesn't look fancy, but the father of one of the girls she helped is a car mechanic. He makes sure it runs perfectly.' Marian had chortled with glee when Callie had commented on the old heap's unexpected turn of speed. It had certainly prevented a nasty stand-off when they'd been trying to get Jodie to safety.

'I just remember you dragging me inside…pulling me with you onto the back seat and telling Marian to get going when Billy… when he…'

Callie glanced sideways at her passenger. She saw the silvery track of a tear on her cheek and the way her hand shook when she reached up to wipe it away.

'You know you're safe now, Jodie,' she reminded her. 'The police took him into custody when he turned up at the hospital to have his hand attended to. He won't be able to hurt you again.'

'So why doesn't the ache go away?' she whispered, and Callie automatically slowed the car.

'You're in pain?' she exclaimed. 'Jodie, why didn't you say something before I took you out of the hospital? You should have stayed until—'

'Not that sort of pain,' she interrupted, her lower lip trembling as she fought for control. 'It's knowing that what he did killed the baby and now it'll never be born or…'

Callie indicated to pull in to the side of the road and switch off the engine, grateful that the traffic was light.

'I know what you mean,' she said quietly. 'You're doing something ordinary like…like having a drink or eating a piece of toast and suddenly you remember that you'll never have the chance to see your child do any of that...no bathtime, no cuddles, no first step, no...'

They were both crying now, but Jodie finally turned her head to look directly at her.

'How can *you* know what it feels like?' she accused. 'You're only a do-gooder; just guessing, trying to make me feel better.'

'I wish I were,' Callie said fervently, the memories ripping open the wound inside her that she didn't think would ever heal. 'But...I lost my baby a few months ago. He died before he could be born.'

'Did your old man knock you about, too?' Jodie asked with the sort of hard look in her eyes that no child her age should ever have.

'No! Never!' Callie exclaimed, horrified by the very idea that Con would raise a hand to her. 'No *decent* man would *ever* hit a woman.' Unfortunately, losing his love had felt every bit as painful as any physical blow, but that wasn't something she was willing to discuss—far safer to stick to the topic in hand.

'They did tests on the baby to see if they could

find out why he died—' and although she'd realised that the autopsy was necessary, she'd died a thousand deaths knowing what was happening to his perfect tiny body '—but they couldn't find anything wrong with him so it was inconclusive.' Except she'd known it meant that the fault must have been *hers*. Her precious baby had died because her faulty body had failed to protect him and nourish him until he had been strong enough to be born.

Perhaps that was why it had been so difficult for her to get pregnant in the first place—because it was never supposed to happen.

Well, she certainly wouldn't be trying again. She couldn't go through that roller-coaster ride of alternating hope and despair again.

Jodie was silent for a long time but Callie had a feeling that she needed this space to process her thoughts. Once they reached The Place there wouldn't be much chance for quiet time on a one-to-one basis.

It took a moment or two before she realised that the youngster was crying again, silent tears streaming down her face.

'Oh, Jodie, sweetheart…' she murmured, at a loss to know just what to do. Her every instinct was telling her to wrap her arms around the traumatised youngster but, having suffered abuse, would she accept such a physical expression of sympathy?

'W-why did it have to die?' she sobbed, wrapping her skinny arms around her own body. 'W-why does everyone I love have to d-die?'

Callie released both seat belts, her decision made. No one should have to try to cope with that much unhappiness without a pair of comforting arms around her.

Jodie stiffened briefly when Callie wrapped an arm around her shoulders and tried to draw her head down onto her shoulder but then collapsed against her in a sudden paroxysm of grief. Callie nearly joined her again, but this was not about venting her own feelings of devastation and loss. This was about helping a young girl come to terms with her own unhappiness.

It was several long heartbroken minutes

before she was ready to accept Callie's offer of a spare handkerchief, gradually subsiding into hiccups and sniffs.

'You won't tell anyone?' she demanded just as Callie was reaching to turn the engine on again. 'I don't want everyone knowing that I lost it, big time.'

Callie suppressed a smile when she heard the uncertain mixture of child and woman revealed by the diffident words and the tough edge in the way she said them.

'Not a word,' she promised. 'Whatever we've said in this car stays there—and that works both ways, OK?'

'You don't want me telling the other girls about you losing your baby?'

'I don't like talking about it…not yet. It's still too soon,' Callie admitted, but whether that was because of the baby himself or the fact that losing him had destroyed her marriage to Con, she didn't know.

Their arrival at The Place was relatively low-key, with most of the present residents away from the house for one reason or another.

Marian had returned—a fact Callie could tell from the clatter of pots and pans and the muttered imprecations coming from behind the firmly closed door.

She didn't bother to hide her grin.

'Let's go and annoy Marian,' she suggested to Josie, dumping the girl's meagre belongings just inside the front door. 'She hates cooking, so when she's in there, the other girls usually steer clear.' She led the way to the door at the other end of the wide hallway.

'If she hates cooking, why does she do it? Couldn't she get someone else to do it?' Jodie asked, but even as she hung back uncertainly in the doorway, Callie could see that she was intrigued.

'I'd get someone else to do it like a shot, if they'd work for nothing,' Marian said as she slashed at a pile of onions with tears streaming down her cheeks, clearly having overheard what Jodie had said. 'They'd also need to be able to cope with anything from two to twelve mouths at a meal and be able to make money stretch like elastic when they do grocery shopping.'

'What are you doing?' Jodie asked as she moved as close as she dared to the oversized knife.

'Chopping onions,' Marian said in disgust, reaching for a sheet of kitchen towel to wipe her streaming eyes and blow her nose vigorously.

'I can see that,' Jodie said with a 'Duh!' intonation. 'But what are the onions for?'

'The recipe says it'll be spaghetti Bolognese when it's finished, but at this rate, it'll be some time around midnight.'

'You'd find it easier to chop the onions into small pieces if you didn't make them into onion rings, first,' Jodie pointed out, suddenly stepping around Marian to wash her hands under the tap then appropriating the discarded vegetable knife on the table. 'Like this,' she said as she swiftly peeled the dried layers off the vegetable, cut it in half from tip to root and lay both halves cut-side-down on the free end of the chopping board. 'Then it's easy to do a series of cuts from root to tip then turn it at right-angles and chop again.'

'Wow!' Marian said as she watched the speed with which Jodie wielded the knife, reducing the onion to a neat pile of even-sized pieces.

'Very impressive,' Callie agreed. 'You've obviously done that before.'

'My gran taught me,' said Jodie as she worked her way efficiently through the rest of the onions. 'She and Grandad had a restaurant and my dad was going to take over when he came out of the army.'

'So what happened?' Callie prompted, hoping she sounded only casually interested as she took the enormous frying pan from Marian and put it on the stove with a swirl of olive oil in the bottom.

'He was killed,' she said bluntly, as she swiped the onions off the chopping board and into the pan. 'So I carried on living with Gran and Grandad.'

'Is that where you live now?' Marian asked. 'Will your grandparents be worrying about you?'

'They're dead, too.' Her tone was flat with resignation. 'The council made a mistake with their property tax and even though they'd always paid everything on time, *they* said they owed thousands and thousands. They didn't!' she exclaimed heatedly. 'They didn't owe a single penny, but Grandad was so worried by it that he had a heart attack and died. Gran couldn't manage the restaurant by herself and she'd started getting very confused and they wanted to take her away and put her in a home. I told them she'd die if they took her away from the place she'd always lived with Grandad, but they wouldn't listen because I'm just a kid.'

Marian and Callie had both stepped aside to leave the youngster room at the stove, their eyes meeting over her head as her diatribe continued, her voice and movements becoming more and more jerky as she stirred the minced meat into the softened onions.

'They shoved me in a home where they treated me like a little kid who had to be watched every minute when *I'd* been the one watching over Gran.' She was silent for several minutes while she sorted through Marian's limited selection of herbs and spices and detailed Callie to open some tins of tomatoes.

'I was only putting up with the home until I was old enough for them to let me go,' she said in a low voice. 'Then I was going to get Gran out of that smelly old people's home and we'd be together again…only…only she died and then…' She faltered momentarily and Callie wondered if she would finally give in to tears again. She'd cried for her baby but had she ever grieved for the loss of her grandparents? Then her chin came up and she continued grimly. 'After that, there wasn't any point in staying around stuck in the system, so I walked out.'

'Hey! Something smells great!' exclaimed a voice from the kitchen door, and the time for confidences was over.

'Yeah! What is it, Marian? A take-away or something out of the supermarket freezer?' demanded another, and had a wet dishcloth thrown at her in retaliation.

'Cheeky madam!' Marian grumbled. 'My cooking's not as bad as that.'

'No, but it doesn't smell as good as this. What is it?'

Callie had been watching Jodie's face while the banter had been going on and saw the fleeting emotions crossing it. She was relieved to see the shadow of sad memories lift a little and saw it replaced with an entirely understandable nervousness at meeting a group of strangers.

'This is Jodie and she's giving me a master class in the cooking of Bolognese sauce,' Marian announced briskly. She made a quick round of introductions but all the other girls were interested in was what Jodie was creating on the stove. Callie was secretly delighted to see the quiet pride that filled the newest member of their group and was determined to see if there was some way that her interest in cooking could be fostered. Perhaps it would provide an important link with the grandparents she'd loved if she were helped to gain qualifications as a chef? She would have to have a word with Marian about that when the girls went to bed that night.

In the meantime, the sauce was ready to be left to simmer while Jodie was taken on a lightning tour of the house and shown to the room she'd been allocated, next to Callie's.

'What a dump!' she exclaimed when she saw the state of the walls and paintwork, and Callie had to admit it suffered by comparison with the rooms the other girls were occupying, even though all the basic repairs and preparation had been done.

'That's what ours looked like after we took all the manky wallpaper off,' one of the other girls reassured her cheerfully. 'Marian helps us to strip each room out and repair it and then we get to choose our own colours when it's time to paint it and make curtains and things.'

'Really?' Jodie looked towards Callie as though for confirmation and when she smiled and nodded, said, 'Cool! When can we start?'

'You're supposed to be taking it easy after your surgery,' Callie pointed out. 'You've only just had your stitches taken out.'

'No problemo!' dismissed one of the girls breezily. 'If we all help a bit, we can do it without anyone hurting themselves. We've just finished Jess's room, ready for when she comes home with the baby. We'll start on yours in the morning, OK?'

'But first it's time to put the pasta on to boil and set the table,' Marian decreed as she began to herd her charges back towards the stairs.

'And whose turn is it to do the washing-up tonight?' She turned to Jodie. 'By the way, before anyone tries to con *you* into doing it, we have an absolute rule here that whoever does the cooking is excused from doing the washing-up.'

Callie followed on with her emotions in turmoil. *This* was what she'd hoped her own home would be like...noisy and full of laughter...but it wasn't to be. She would have to come to terms with the fact that she would never have the big boisterous family she'd always dreamed of.

The Place had been a lifeline in the few days since she'd finally admitted that she was standing in the way of Con's happiness. Perhaps her involvement here would go some way to filling the aching void inside her until she could decide what to do with the rest of her life.

And making a decision wasn't going to be easy when she couldn't visualise a life without Con in it.

CHAPTER FIVE

'MARTIN, there must be *something* more I can do!' Con exclaimed, his hands so tightly clasped around the whisky glass his friend had given him that his knuckles gleamed white.

Not that he'd drunk any of the stuff. He'd only accepted it because it gave him something to look at instead of staring at another four walls.

'I'm sorry, Con, but I can't—'

'Oh, I know you wouldn't tell me anything even if you could,' Con interrupted sharply, still piqued by the fact that Martin had informed him that he would be acting on Callie's behalf in the event that the two of them divorced. The two of them had been friends for so many years that he'd automatically assumed that Martin would be on *his* side in any dispute.

Not that there was going to be a divorce, not

if he had anything to say about it. Still, there was a strange sort of comfort in knowing that Callie would have a man she could trust in her corner. 'You've always been a straight arrow, Martin, so I know there's no point in even asking you to tell me where she is.'

'It would come under the heading of client confidentiality, if I *did* know where she was staying,' Martin agreed. 'But, Con, I'm being perfectly honest with you when I tell you that she hasn't been in contact again. Not once since that initial phone call.'

'Then there was that sighting at that hospital on the other side of the country,' Con reminded him. 'But when I rang, they were adamant that they didn't have a Dr Lowell on staff. Anyway, it was unlikely that it was anything to do with Callie at all.'

'Why not?' Martin asked. 'I would have thought that the role of good Samaritan suited her perfectly. That paramedic said that she'd helped a youngster who'd been mugged and that sounds exactly like the sort of thing that Callie would do.'

'But not in the middle of a city,' Con pointed out. 'She couldn't wait to move out to a more rural area as soon as we'd qualified. She said she couldn't breathe properly when she was completely surrounded by buildings.'

'Perhaps that was because she was already thinking ahead to being in a good place to bring up a family,' Martin suggested gently, but to Con the pang of loss was still agonising at the reminder of all the two of them had lost. 'Perhaps,' his friend continued inexorably, 'the fact that she wasn't able to have the children you wanted made her decide to move some-where completely different, so she wouldn't always be reminded of…'

'Dammit, I didn't only want her for the children she might or might not give me,' Con exploded, barely resisting the temptation to smash the crystal tumbler into the fireplace. 'It was *Callie* I wanted, *Callie* I love, *Callie* I'm missing…' His throat closed and he couldn't speak for a moment while he fought the urge to cry like a baby.

'Listen, I've got all sorts of people keeping

their ears to the ground,' Martin promised. 'I know you've been keeping an eye on any A and E posts coming up and checking to see who's been appointed...although I'm not absolutely certain that your methods would bear scrutiny.'

'I'll do whatever it takes to find out where she's gone,' Con said fervently, weeks of exhaustion weighing heavily on his shoulders. 'And I won't care if I'm breaking the law, either. She's my wife and she's been through hell and I need to know that she's well and she's safe. I also need to meet her face to face to find out why she left me like that. I need to know if it was something I said...something I did...or something I *didn't* say or do that I *should* have. I just can't leave it until I *know*.'

Not that he'd be willing to let her go even then, he admitted silently. Callie was the only woman he'd ever loved—the only woman he *would* ever love—and he'd be a fool if he didn't fight for her.

But to fight for her, first he had to find her.

'I can't understand how she could disappear so completely,' he said aloud. 'It's as if she just vanished into thin air once she left the house.

Nobody saw her leaving. She didn't order a taxi. She hasn't once used a cheque or a piece of plastic so we can find out what area she's gone to.'

'On the good side, the police pointed out that at least it means that she hasn't been admitted to a hospital after an accident and she hasn't been robbed, with someone going on a spending spree with her cards.'

'But what is she living on?' Con demanded, worry amounting anew. 'We didn't have any more than a couple of hundred in the house before she left, and if she's paying for accommodation somewhere, that must be long gone.'

'So, she's an intelligent woman who's found herself somewhere inexpensive to stay,' Martin said, obviously trying hard to raise Con's spirits. 'And she's possibly found some sort of job where they'll pay her in cash so she isn't having to take anything out of the bank.'

'Dammit! Where *is* she?' Con demanded, frustration at his inability to do anything about the situation mixed with the underlying fear that he might never see her again.

He wouldn't ever voice those words aloud. That would seem too much like tempting fate. But it was a nightmare that was waking him more and more frequently as the days grew into weeks, and if the weeks stretched into months…?

Surely, at some stage, she would have to contact Martin, if only to find out whether the paperwork necessary for the divorce she wanted was ready for her signature.

Or, was the fact that she hadn't been in contact a *good* sign? Did it mean that she was reluctant to find out that he had given in and instructed Martin to go ahead? Now that she'd had some time to think, was she regretting leaving? Had she changed her mind about the divorce? Was she trying to find some way to return without losing too much face?

As if he would do anything other than welcome her back with open arms!

'I'm going to go mad if I don't get some sleep soon,' he muttered, then brought the glass to his lips and gulped the liquid back in a single swallow.

'That's the last time I give you any of my

precious single malt,' Martin grumbled, even as it was burning a fiery path all the way down to Con's empty stomach.

'Sorry, mate, but I'm not exactly in the mood to savour it,' he admitted as he forced himself to his feet, feeling closer to ninety-four than thirty-four. 'I've got to get home. I'm on an early start tomorrow morning.' And he needed to be there just in case Callie should try to phone. He didn't think he could bear it if he were to walk in the front door and see the light blinking to tell him she'd had to leave a message because he hadn't been there to speak to her in person.

Even so, as he put the key in the lock, he found himself holding his breath until he swung the door open saw by the steady light on the telephone under the hall mirror that there were no messages waiting. Then he completed the rest of his pathetic ritual, standing silently in the middle of the hallway and listening, hoping against hope to hear some ordinary little sound that would tell him that Callie had come back and the house wasn't achingly empty and lonely any more.

Nothing.

Not a sound barring the distant muted hum of the refrigerator and the tick-tick as the boiler cooled after switching off for the night. There would be hot water for his shower tonight and enough spare to put a load of bedding through the washing machine.

It had nearly brought him to tears the first time he'd done it, knowing he was going to be washing away any lingering traces of the scent of Callie's skin. There had been a comforting feeling that she wasn't so far away when he'd gone to bed and felt himself surrounded by her essence. He'd almost resorted to dabbing some of her favourite perfume on the clean pillowcase but sanity had prevailed at the last moment. The scent of her perfume in their bed was no substitute for the presence of a living, breathing, loving woman in his arms.

'You're looking so tired,' crooned Sonja when she came upon him in the staffroom, and Con could have screamed aloud. He'd just managed to drop off for a few minutes after a killer night on duty and the stupid woman couldn't leave him alone.

'You'll give yourself a stiff neck sleeping in a chair like that,' she scolded, almost as though he were a five-year old. She walked behind the chair and he breathed a sigh of relief.

Too soon.

He nearly leapt into the air when, instead of going across to make herself a cup of coffee, she placed both hands on his shirt-covered shoulders and began to massage his aching muscles.

'Don't!' he snapped, as he thrust himself out of the chair and out of her grasp, feeling strangely violated by her unwanted attentions.

'But it would make you feel so much better,' she insisted, approaching him again. 'I don't like to see you in pain. Please, let me help you. I'm very good at giving…therapeutic massages.'

'No, thank you,' he said firmly, repulsed by the suggestive twist she'd given the term, and gave up all hope of any sort of break, opting for returning hastily to the business end of the department…anywhere where there were plenty of people he could use as a buffer between himself and the increasingly pushy nurse.

What on earth had got into the woman? It

wasn't as if he'd made any advances to her. Why would he when he loved Callie? Anyway, the woman had a reputation as a bit of a man-eater with her venal soul fixed on the idea of marrying a doctor come what may. Thank goodness he was one of the married ones, so she couldn't seriously be targeting him.

Anyway, he thought dismissively as he pulled back the curtain on the cubicle where his next patient was sitting waiting for a nerve-blocking injection before his injury was cleaned, debrided and sutured, the woman was totally unimportant in comparison with his worry about Callie.

'Callie…can I talk to you?'

Callie looked up from the fiddly job of pinning the gathering tape to the top of a curtain ready for machining and smiled, only too willing to have something other than her thoughts of Con to concentrate on. 'Of course you can, Debs. What's on your mind?'

The youngster reached out for the pincushion and concentrated fiercely on taking each one out in turn and replacing them in a pattern of concentric circles—a classic sign of someone trying to create order in the midst of the chaos of their lives.

Callie stayed silent, giving the girl time to start the conversation, and was rewarded for her patience when suddenly the pincushion was tossed onto the table.

'I don't know what to do,' she wailed as she slumped onto the nearby chair. 'My baby's due in a few weeks and I still don't know what's best.'

'Go on,' Callie encouraged with a smile.

'Well, that's it, really,' she said unhappily. 'I know there are scads of people who want to adopt and Marian would help to make certain they'd been checked out…that they'd be good for the baby and would love it…but…'

'But?' Callie prompted when the silence looked as if it would stretch for ever.

'But I couldn't bear it…not seeing my baby ever again. Not knowing if it was happy or sad or…' She shook her head impatiently. 'I know I'm too young and it'd be hard to look after it while I'm all on my own but…but it's mine and I already love it and…'

'Hey! Hey! Take it easy, Debs,' Callie soothed. 'You don't have to make a decision today and you don't have to do it all by yourself…unless you want to.' She reached for a nearby box of tissues, just in case the threatened tears started to fall. 'Have you tried doing the "pros and cons" list Marian was talking about the other day?'

'I started,' she admitted, and fished a decidedly crumpled sheet of paper from the pocket of her oversized jeans. 'The trouble is, I'm not sure which list some things belong on—like my age, for example. I'm seventeen—just—but is that a good thing because it means I'm young and energetic… usually,' she added with a grimace towards her swollen waistline. 'Or is it a bad thing because I'm not old enough to know how to take care of a baby?'

'It's probably both, which is why you're having trouble working out the best thing to do.' Callie thought for a moment before she broached a topic that could open up all sorts of wounds for some of their girls. 'I think one of the biggest problems about being a single parent is just the fact that you're on your own.'

'Well, my parents certainly don't want to have anything to do with me or the baby,' she snapped. 'They more or less washed their hands of me when I said I wasn't going to go into law, like the two of them.'

'You're joking!' Callie exclaimed, remembering the endless support her own family had given her. If they had still been around now…

'I wish I were,' the youngster said softly. 'They seemed to think that just because they were my parents, that gave them the right to dictate what I was going to do with my life, and as I was intelligent enough to pass the exams to get into law school—a foregone conclusion with them as my parents, of course—I had an absolute duty to go.'

'And what did you want to do?'

'I wasn't sure,' she admitted. 'All I knew was that I didn't want to be a lawyer who was always so busy and under so much pressure that they didn't have time for their own daughter.'

'And you didn't think that, knowing how

much you'd hated it, you wouldn't have made certain to be a completely *different* sort of lawyer?' Callie suggested, the information that Debs came from lawyer parents making perfect sense when she remembered the way Debs had mediated between two of their residents earlier on in the day. 'I don't know much about the legal profession, but aren't there lots of different branches, like contract law and family law and so on?'

'Yes…' she said thoughtfully, then shook her head firmly. 'But it's useless thinking about it now. There's no way I could ever go to law school while I've got a tiny baby, and I couldn't bear the thought of putting my child into day care for months at a time while I…' She stopped talking suddenly and fixed Callie with an exasperated glare. 'How did you do that?' she demanded.

'Do what?' Callie asked innocently.

'You know!' Debs accused. 'You got me talking about… about everything! About my parents…about the way they tried to force me to do what they wanted…about…' She shook her head.

'Did it help you to see things differently, coming at it from a slightly different angle?' Callie asked. 'Might it help you to come to any decisions?'

'Yes…and no,' the young woman said thoughtfully. 'It made me realise that I really want to keep my baby, because I know that I'll love it and take care of it well.' She pulled a face and her shoulders slumped before she continued. 'But I also know that will mean that I have very little chance of ever having a worthwhile career.'

'Why do you say that?'

'Well, it's obvious, isn't it? I won't be able to afford to pay my tuition fees even if I get a place to study law, let alone support the two of us.'

Callie bit her tongue at the tacit admission that the girl was still thinking about a legal career, in spite of her vehement opposition to the idea when it had been forced on her. She was longing to make an obvious suggestion, but was it something that Debs would have to come to on her own?

'Callie? Do you think my parents would ever

forgive me?' she asked quietly, and Callie gave a silent cheer.

'Do you think you would be able to forgive *your* child?' she countered.

'Of course,' Debs said, without needing to pause a single second for thought, then she sent Callie a dawning smile that only wobbled a bit at the corners, her eyes suspiciously bright. 'Please, will you come to the office with me while I ring them?' she begged. 'I don't know if I could bear it if they slammed the phone down on me.'

'Of course I will,' Callie said, knowing just how hard it was to find the courage to make that fatal call. She'd been putting off contacting Martin for far too long, but she just couldn't bear the thought of speaking to him and finding out that Con had signed all the papers ready for their divorce. All the time she didn't hear the fact that he was waiting for her signature, she could pretend that it wasn't happening…that the two of them were still married and had a chance of reconciling.

'Can I speak to Mr Glasson, please?' Callie

said when a very efficient-sounding woman answered the phone.

'This is Mrs Glasson. Can I help you?' she said, and Callie realised she was speaking to Debs's mother.

'Mrs Glasson, do you have a daughter called Debs… Deborah?' she asked, and heard a gasp on the other end.

'You've seen her?' the woman demanded. 'You've seen my daughter? Where is she? Is she all right?' The questions were being fired at her thick and fast and the concern in her voice was obvious even to Debs as Callie held the phone between them so the youngster could hear, too.

'Mrs Glasson, your daughter is here. Would you like to speak to her?'

'Yes!' she said eagerly. 'Oh, yes, *please…*' Then added with an unexpected touch of hesitation, 'If she still wants to speak to me.'

Callie held the phone out again, unsurprised to see that the teenager's hand was shaking as she took it.

'M-Mum?' she said with a definite hiccup in her voice. 'I'm s-sorry.'

'No, darling, *I'm* sorry,' Callie heard her mother interrupt. 'Your father and I *both* are for trying to push you so hard…' The rest of the conversation was lost to Callie as she closed the door on her way out of the room.

'I take it there's the possibility of a reconciliation?' Marian asked softly, and Callie jumped. She hadn't realised that the other woman had been waiting in the corridor.

'A definite possibility, if her mother's eagerness to talk to her is any guide,' Callie said. 'Hopefully that's one down and how many thousands more to go before we've made all the homeless girls safe.'

'Are you sure you aren't a qualified counsellor?' Marian asked as they made their way to the kitchen by silent mutual consent.

Callie laughed the suggestion off but inside was asking, If I were, would my own life be in such a mess? Somehow it seemed so much easier to see the way through other people's problems than her own.

'There was no guarantee that Debs's mother wanted to speak to her,' Callie pointed out.

'There are plenty who are quite happy to wash their hands of their daughters.' She didn't have to mention Steph by name for the two of them to know who she meant. Under her 'Whatever!' attitude was a young girl breaking her heart that her mother cared for her so little that she wouldn't take her part against a lecherous stepfather.

'If I had my way, the man would be castrated,' Marian muttered, proving that her thoughts had been running along the same lines. 'That's the only punishment that will stop rapists and paedophiles re-offending…the same way some countries punish a thief by cutting his hand off.'

'Not that it's in any way a radical suggestion, of course,' Callie teased, 'especially when some men are deliberately wrongfully accused by a girl who has second thoughts after the event.'

'Yes, well, there might be some *small* flaws in my solution,' Marian admitted wryly.

'To say nothing of the fact that most judges are men and would be unlikely to impose such a sentence,' Callie pointed out. 'You only have to mention someone getting their private parts caught in a zip to see men look sick. Having it cut off? Well…'

'All right, I concede,' Marian said as she gestured towards the last small piece of apple turnover with a raised eyebrow.

Callie shook her head. 'You have it,' she said. Jodie's dessert had been a smash hit with the residents, so much so that it was surprising to see any left over, but there must have been something about the cinnamon that she'd dusted over the pastry that hadn't agreed with her because she was feeling slightly nauseous. It was either that or the fact that her conversation with Debs had made her see her own situation from a different angle, leaving her wondering if she'd made a massive mistake when she'd walked away from Con like that. 'I think I might go out for a few minutes of fresh air.'

'Well, if you're going in the garden, beware of the brambles at face height,' Marian warned as an expression of bliss crossed her face when she took a bite of the pastry. 'I haven't had time to do anything with it out there. It seemed more important to do the living accommodation first.'

Callie had her hand on the catch but hadn't even had time to release it when she heard the sudden thunder of feet hurrying down the stairs.

'Marian. Callie. Come quick. She's bleeding,' shouted a voice in the hallway.

'Who's bleeding?' demanded Marian as they both took off at a run.

'Where is she bleeding from, and for how long?' demanded Callie as she followed Marian up the stairs two at a time.

'Francine, and she says it's like a period but it can't be because she's pregnant,' Sue said as she puffed in their wake, unable to go up the stairs quite as fast as she'd come down.

'Francine, sweetheart,' Marian said as she hurried across to the white-faced youngster curled up in her dressing-gown on the end of her bed.

'How long have you been bleeding?' Callie demanded as she knelt on the rug beside the bed and held the girl's wrist in one hand while she pushed her tangled dark hair off her clammy forehead with the other. Francine's pulse was faster than she would have liked, but whether that was due to fear or was an indicator of serious blood loss...

'It started this morning, just a little bit, and I remember someone telling me that you could get spotting even when you were pregnant...but it's more than that, I think.'

'Have you had any pains or done anything particularly strenuous today?' Callie asked, wishing she had just a few items of the vast selection of diagnostic equipment that would have been available to her in St Mark's A and E department. A sphyg and an ultrasound machine would be her first choices at the moment.

'No pains until...' She paused, looking rather shame-faced.

'Out with it, missy,' Marian ordered. 'What have you been up to?'

'I moved some furniture,' she admitted tearfully. 'I just wanted to see if the room looked any better, and if there'd be enough room for a baby's cot in here if I changed things round a bit.'

'So, why didn't you ask for some help?'

Marian was clearly exasperated. 'You know I warned all of you not to do the heavy stuff.'

'Have I hurt my baby?' the youngster sobbed. 'Have I killed it?'

'How many weeks are you?' Callie asked, sticking to the important facts rather than trying to answer the impossible. 'When is your baby due?'

'Not for a month…well, four weeks and a bit. That's much too soon. I can't be in labour!' Panic was clearly taking over, especially when she glanced down and saw the bright blood pooling beneath her.

'Marian, will you make a phone call?' Callie asked. 'I think Francine might have caused a little tear inside when she was moving her furniture.' The way Marian's eyes widened told her that the older woman had understood the potential urgency of the situation. If, as she suspected, they were dealing with a placental abruption, it wasn't just the baby's life that could be hanging in the balance. This rate of blood loss could threaten the young mother, too.

It was frustrating to have to sit calmly on the

edge of the bed and hold a soothing conversation with the girl when she would far rather be setting up an IV to replace the fluids she was losing.

'Ow! That hurts!' Francine moaned, and Callie placed her hand beside the youngster's where it cradled the curve of her swollen abdomen.

A contraction, she realised, even as she noted the extra flow of blood it caused. If that ambulance didn't arrive soon…

'They're coming,' Marian said as she hurried back into the room. 'Where do you keep your wash things, sweetheart? And which drawer do you keep your nighties in?'

Callie was grateful for the woman's non-stop chatter as she collected Francine's essentials, glad that it was taking the girl's mind off her situation, but she was absolutely delighted to hear the familiar sound of a siren growing closer just a moment or two later.

'She's up here,' she heard Sue call from her self-imposed sentry duty at the top of the stairs when the paramedic entered the hallway below, the front door having been opened by Debs, who'd been detailed to make sure they knew they'd come to the right house.

'Hello, my lovely. What have you been doing to yourself?' asked the paramedic as he took Marian's place beside Francine.

Callie itched to supply all the answers he needed, but having a conscious patient speak to him was an important part of his assessment of the situation.

'I'm bleeding. I moved some furniture and Callie says I might have torn something inside,' Francine told him in a shaky voice.

'And are you in any pain?' he asked after a muttered aside to his colleague for an IV, and Callie allowed herself to relax a little. It was obvious that he'd quickly grasped the potential danger of the situation.

'I had a pain a few minutes ago, but nothing mo—Ow! It's happening again,' she whimpered.

'It's possible that it's placental abruption,' Callie murmured as she watched his smooth technique for setting up the IV. She doubted she could have done it any better herself. 'Her pulse is rapid and she's pale and clammy, and with each contraction there's an increase in blood loss.'

'Oh, hi!' he said with a smile of recognition, and she realised it was Mike, the same paramedic who had attended Steph after she'd been mugged. 'We shall have to stop meeting like this.'

There wasn't much time for conversation after that, all their attention focused on helping Francine into the stretcher-chair and transferring her as swiftly as possible to the back of the ambulance where she could lie down again.

'You go with her,' Marian urged. 'Just in case she needs extra help before she gets to the hospital.'

'She doesn't know me as well as she knows you,' Callie pointed out. 'And anyway, I wouldn't be able to do anything for her in the back of a speeding ambulance.' But Marian insisted, and within seconds the double doors were locked and the engine started with the siren beginning to wail as soon as their wheels hit the road.

CHAPTER SIX

'WHAT have you got?' demanded Con, as the paramedics pushed the trolley swiftly up the ramp from the ambulance bay and into the department.

'This is Sarah Wagner. She's twenty-nine years old and in her thirty-fourth week of pregnancy. Possible placental abruption,' said the female paramedic as she stood back to allow the A and E staff to transfer her patient off the trolley and onto the hospital's monitoring systems. 'She had a fall while hanging curtains in the baby's nursery. Started bleeding shortly after. She's cold and clammy and her pulse and respirations are climbing. She's losing frank blood. We've put two IVs in, running wide open, and put her on Entonox, but left everything else to get here as quickly as possible.'

'Good call,' Con muttered as he saw the first

results on the monitors. 'Do you know where she was due to give birth? And when? Have we got her medical history in the hospital system? And tell somebody to get hold of Obs and Gyn. Tell them we need them here—now!'

The thought that this poor woman might be about to lose her precious baby at this late stage of her pregnancy was almost crippling him, but there was no way that he could allow himself to do anything less than his best for her.

One of the monitors began shrilling a warning and he saw that her blood pressure was plummeting. It looked as if there wasn't even going to be time to transfer her up to Theatre.

'Where's my wife?' demanded a voice full of terror outside the trauma suite. 'She's having a baby and had a fall. Does anyone know where she is?'

A quick glance over his mask sent one of the nurses hurrying out to find out if this was their patient's husband. Her condition was worsening so quickly that he didn't dare make the man wait outside the room, no matter how gory things might look. It might be his last chance to see his wife alive, and as for their baby...

Memories of the moment when the lifeless body of his tiny son had been placed in his arms suddenly rose up in front of him and the pain was devastating. For a moment he could barely breathe but then a voice right beside him said, 'This is Andrew Wagner, Sarah's husband,' and he had to shut the memories away.

'Push those fluids in,' he ordered. 'How long before we get some cross-matched blood?' Then he turned to greet the terrified man hovering behind him.

'What's happening?' Andrew demanded, his eyes wide with panic. 'They said Sarah fell off the ladder. Has she broken her leg? Has something happened to the baby?'

'It looks as if the fall has torn something inside,' Con said, unable to find any other way of explaining the situation in the limited time available. 'She's bleeding badly and we're going to have to do an emergency Caesarean section to get the baby out.'

'But... You can't! It's too soon!' he exclaimed, his eyes flicking frantically backwards and forwards between Con and his unconscious wife. 'It's not due for another six weeks.'

'If we don't operate immediately, your wife probably won't be alive in six *minutes*,' Con said bluntly, grateful when one of the more experienced nurses took the grey-faced man by the elbow and started to lead him out of the room.

At the last moment he pulled away and strode swiftly towards the unconscious figure on the trolley. Con stiffened, wondering if he was going to have a fight on his hands to be allowed to do the life-saving operation, then had to swallow a lump in his throat when the man cupped a gentle hand around his wife's face and bent to brush a kiss over her cheek, beside the oxygen mask.

'I love you,' he saw the man say, the words totally inaudible over the frantic sounds of activity in the room, and then he strode away again and out of the room, as straight-backed as a man on his way to a firing squad.

'How long before Eric Benton gets here?' he

demanded, when the monitors told him that they were barely keeping pace with the woman's blood loss no matter how fast they pushed the replacement fluids in. 'Which paediatrician is on duty...and where is Frank Oakley?'

'I'm here,' said a deep voice as the squat figure of the tubby anaesthetist shouldered his way into the room. 'Tell me what's going on.'

By the time Con had brought him up to date with Sarah Wagner's situation the man had calculated the correct doses of the appropriate anaesthetic drugs and was ready to administer them.

Another monitor shrilled out a warning and Con swore aloud and turned towards the nearby sink.

'Swearing won't work,' Frank said firmly as he pushed the first drug into the port on the back of their patient's limp hand, swiftly followed by the second. 'You can't afford to wait for Benton or Wheal to get here or we'll lose her.'

Con had already come to the same conclusion and was scrubbing even as the anaesthetic started to take her deep enough so that the pain of the incision would never be felt.

By the time he turned back to the trolley freshly scrubbed, gowned and gloved, someone had opened the kit prepared for an emergency Caesarean and everything was readily to hand.

'Ready?' he asked with a quick glance towards the anaesthetist.

'As she'll ever be,' he agreed. 'But her BP's on the floor, so don't waste time doing anything fancy. Just get in there and stop the bleeding… fast!'

'You started without me,' complained a breathless voice as the doors slapped shut behind a new figure.

'Catch your breath while you get some gloves on,' growled Con as he made a swift midline incision over the increasingly rigid mound from epigastrium to pubic symphysis. He started the second vertical incision through the wall of the uterus, and breathed a sigh of gratitude that the placenta was attached elsewhere. If it had been in the surgical field, the need for speed would have necessitated making the incision directly through the placenta and the blood loss would have increased exponentially. 'But scrub fast because this is going to be a two-man job.'

It was a race against time with the spectre of shock, kidney failure and brain death hanging over the young woman as they swiftly removed the baby from her womb, hanging it head down below the level of the mother's abdomen so that it received as much of the cord blood as possible into its tiny system until the placenta was clamped and cut.

The baby looked frighteningly still as it was whisked away to the other side of the room, its colour that strange mixture of grey and purple that would only change to healthy pink when it took in that life-giving surge of oxygen with its first gasping breath.

Except it wasn't making a sound yet, no matter how frantically the paediatric consultant was working on it...but Con didn't have time to break his heart over another dead baby when there was a woman still fighting for her life. Thank goodness Eric Benton had seen many more of these situations than he had and had already ordered the administration of the drug that would shut down the blood vessels supplying the placenta and trigger it to peel away from the wall of the uterus. With any luck, the haemorrhage should stop spontaneously as the placenta separated, and the patient's blood volume would start to rise.

He wouldn't allow himself to contemplate the worst-case scenario unless it became unavoidable. The last thing they wanted to do was to have to remove the woman's uterus, especially as it looked as if her baby wasn't going to survive.

'It's not looking good, guys,' warned the anaesthetist, his eyes fixed on the readouts from the various monitors as he manually squeezed two units of blood to speed them down the lines into his patient's veins.

Eric Benton grunted, his concentration too acute to formulate a reply. There weren't really any words needed to confirm that he was moving as fast as he could to find out where the blood was coming from and to stop it as soon as possible.

Con was relegated to providing suction to clear the area, and there was a frightening amount of blood draining away. It seemed almost impossible that one slender female could possibly lose so much and still have a viable heartbeat.

The weak gurgling cry at the other side of the room was just the spur they all needed.

'How's it looking?' Con called over his shoulder.

Chris Wheal looked up from the flailing bundle that was now objecting to his treatment with vigour. 'One little girl has decided she wants to make a go of it,' he announced, and they could all hear the wide smile hidden behind his mask. 'I'm taking her up to NICU. Let me know…'

'We will,' Con said grimly, as the monitor shrilled again as the result of a spate of ectopic beats. How much more could the poor woman's cardiac system stand? There was barely enough blood in it for her heart to beat, let alone keep her brain and organs perfused.

'Got it!' Eric exclaimed as he lifted the placenta out in both hands and deposited it in the bowl that magically appeared in just the right place. 'Will somebody check that the wretched thing is intact while I look…?' The words died away as he peered through the gaping incision, searching for any evidence that she was still bleeding.

Con relinquished the suction probe to Eric and personally double-checked the placenta for any ragged edges. The last thing they needed was pieces of tissue being left in the uterus to set up infection in the days ahead…always presuming the poor woman survived.

'Placenta looks good,' he confirmed, his words colliding with Frank's and Eric's, as both exclaimed their satisfaction.

'I can't see any more bleeding,' announced one.

'BP's coming up,' pronounced the other cautiously, adding, 'Now, get her stitched up, pronto, and let me take her up to ICU.'

Con didn't feel as if he'd taken a full breath in the last hour when he saw the trolley disappear into the lift.

He circled his shoulders one by one, certain he could hear them creaking. That had been far too close for comfort, and it wasn't as if either mother or child was entirely out of the woods yet.

Sarah Wagner's whole system would need time to recover from such traumatic surgery, the enormous blood loss and replacement a concern in itself.

Her daughter, too, had a struggle ahead. Granted, she'd only been born six weeks prematurely, when some born at twenty-eight weeks survived and grew into normal healthy children, but her lungs weren't ready yet to take on the job of providing her body with the oxygen it needed and her skin was so tissue-paper thin that he'd been able to see every tiny vein right through it.

His son had looked even more fragile and, because he'd never drawn that first breath, his skin had never lost that dusky blue hue, the covering of vernix that coated him having made him look almost like a waxen doll.

'Con?' said a voice at his elbow, and he forced himself to shut the memories away as he turned to the junior sister waiting to speak to him. 'Mr Wagner is in the relatives' room, waiting to hear. Do you want me to do the honours?'

'It's all right, Priss. I'll do it,' he said, already

wondering just how cautious he should be in his explanation. 'Any chance of some tea or coffee to take in with me?'

'Give me a second while you clean up,' she suggested with a glance at his blood-stained clothing. 'You'll terrify the man to death if you walk in like that. He'll think they both died on the table.'

'At least he's in with a chance,' Con said as weariness suddenly descended on him like an enormous weight. He began to strip off his disposables with the ease of long practice and deposited the green cotton surgical gown in the laundry bin. 'When Sarah Wagner was first wheeled in I wouldn't have given you odds on her survival...or the baby's.' And just because he was exhausted to the marrow of his bones was no excuse for the feeling of envy he felt that this little family now had a chance at a long and happy life together.

'It's so small,' Francine whispered as she peered into the clear plastic crib that held her newborn child. 'I'm afraid to touch it, in case I hurt it.'

'*It*?' Callie teased. 'You can't go on saying that now he's here.'

'He!' Francine said with a happy grin that was only slightly dimmed by the ordeal she'd undergone. 'I had a *boy*!'

'Have you decided what you're going to call him?' Callie asked, amazed at the youngster's resilience. She couldn't imagine being half as chirpy the day after an emergency Caesarean.

Luckily, the abruption hadn't been as bad as she'd feared, but it had still necessitated several units of blood to replace what she'd lost, and her baby arriving sooner than expected.

'Craig,' she said proudly.

'That's a strong-sounding name. Is he named after someone in your family?'

Francine shook her head. 'I was reading through a book of baby names and I just liked it.' She bit her lip but before Callie could ask her what was worrying her she spoke again. 'Will he be all right?' she asked softly, suddenly looking much older than her years. 'There was a programme on the telly about premature babies having cerebral palsy and never being able to walk or talk. I couldn't bear it if I did that to my baby just because I didn't want to wait for someone to move the furniture around.'

'Everything's fine at the moment,' she reassured her. 'The paediatrician did a whole load of tests and, apart from the fact that Craig is premature, he's doing very well. He's even a pretty good size.'

'A good size!' she exclaimed in disbelief. 'He's *tiny*!'

'But no smaller than some full-term babies— especially multiple births—and they eventually catch up with the rest. It can take years sometimes, and they might need some extra help or be a bit slower than their classmates to do things like walk and talk… That's not to say that things can't go wrong,' she pointed out, not wanting to give the girl too rosy a picture. It would be cruel to let her think that everything would automatically go well. 'Some babies have bleeds in their brain, some have problems with their breathing or their heart…there's just no way of knowing how the next few days and weeks will go.'

It was only after their conversation that Callie

realised she was shaking and spent the whole of the journey back to Marian's place fruitlessly going over everything she'd done in those last days before she'd discovered that her baby had died inside her.

Con had told her not to torture herself with such thoughts, pointing out that there was often no rhyme or reason why it happened…only now thoughts of Con couldn't provide the reassuring comfort they had in the past; now they only brought further pain as she wondered what he was doing, where he was going, and who he was with.

Several times she'd reached out for the phone and once she'd even begun to dial his number, desperate just to hear his voice. Then she imagined how it would sound if there was none of the usual welcoming warmth flowing towards her down the line, or, even worse, if a female voice were to answer, and she couldn't bear to find out. It would be far less painful to speak to Martin if she was going to find out that the divorce papers had all been drawn up and just needed her signature for their marriage to be over.

In her hand she held a much-folded piece of paper, with a line down the centre separating the lists headed pro and con. As she'd drawn it up, she'd discovered—as Debs had—that so many items belonged under both headings.

The fact that she loved Con, for instance, was the best reason in the world for going back to him as soon as possible to see if they could work their way through their problems. But it was also the reason why she'd left him, knowing that if he loved someone else, she wouldn't want to hurt him by trying to hang on to him.

Finally, she'd come to the inescapable conclusion that she shouldn't have left him without talking to him, and that it was a situation that needed to be remedied as soon as possible so the could both get on with their lives. Whether those lives would be spent together or…

'Are you losing weight?' Marian said sternly from the doorway, and Callie wondered just how long she'd been standing there. She'd been so absorbed in her thoughts that she hadn't realised there was anyone about.

'I don't think I've lost any,' Callie said defensively as she folded the list away, knowing that the waistband of her jeans fitted her just as snugly as ever. She still hadn't lost that extra couple of pounds of podge over her belly since…

'Well, your face definitely looks thinner. You've got hollows under your cheekbones and shadows under your eyes,' Marian countered. 'You're not sleeping properly and you're working like a demon all day…outside in the garden whenever the weather's good enough and inside the rest of the time, often late into the evening. Don't think I haven't heard you.'

'The work needs doing,' Callie pointed out stubbornly, keeping to herself the fact that, far from stopping her thinking, the constant physical activity actually seemed to be helping her to think about her situation logically.

'Not at the expense of your health,' Marian insisted, then hesitated a moment before she came over to perch on the corner of the desk where Callie sat. 'Don't think I'm not grateful, Callie, because I am—you'll never know how much.

'And it's not only because you've got a real gift for working with the girls,' she continued when Callie would have interrupted. 'It's the house, too. Not only am I miles ahead of schedule on the work inside the place, but the front garden actually looks welcoming now that the weeds are gone and there are some flowers around the door. And the back seems twice the size without all those brambles, the sort of place where you can see the potential for sitting out with a cup of tea on a sunny day rather than closing your eyes and looking the other way.'

'As I said, it needed doing, and I've never been much good at sitting and twiddling my thumbs if there's work to be done,' Callie said dismissively, loath to reveal just what a life-saver the back-breaking work had been. With a house full of girls chattering around her it was impossible to brood on all the things that might have been. She was having to live in the eternal *now* of a group of youngsters. But out in the garden…

'Just as long as you remember that the same rules apply to you as to the girls,' Marian said sternly. 'You've heard me say it to them often enough—*You are responsible for taking care of yourself, otherwise you can't nurture the baby inside you*—and it's just as important for adult doctors as for runaway teens.'

Callie forbore from pointing out that there was one enormous difference…she wasn't the pregnant one and so could take a few more liberties with the strenuousness of the work she undertook.

'Point taken,' she conceded. 'But sometimes I have to get up and do something when my brain won't switch off and let me sleep.'

'If you want something to occupy your brain, there's plenty of paperwork you could get your teeth into,' Marian groaned, and pointed to the stack beside Callie's elbow. 'There are huge numbers of forms to fill in to apply for grants and charitable bequests, and they take for ever to do. If you've got time on your hands, feel free to dive in. I just can't find enough hours in the day to keep up with it all.'

'You reckon that'll be a sure-fire cure for insomnia?' Callie asked teasingly, knowing how much the financial aspects of starting such a refuge must be hanging over the poor woman's head, but Marian wasn't about to be sidetracked.

'I think the only sure-fire cure will be sorting out your thoughts and feelings,' she said seriously as she straightened up and prepared to leave the cramped little office. 'Running away from them doesn't do any good because they always travel with you wherever you go.'

She was right, Callie had to admit in the middle of another long dark sleepless night. At some stage she was going to have to stop being a coward and face the thing that haunted her.

Not the death of her baby. Devastating as that had been, half of her had never really believed that it would ever be born safely, so, in a way, she'd been expecting something dreadful to happen.

The unthinkable thing that was carving a hollow in her chest where her heart should be was the realisation that she'd lost Con's love.

Oh, he'd tried to reassure her, more than once...to make her believe that the fact she couldn't carry his child didn't matter as long as he had her. But with the twenty-twenty vision of hindsight, she could see that he hadn't been happy, unable even to bring himself to make love with her after that tentative first time, even though weeks had passed since the baby's birth.

Weeks? It had been more like months, and the thought that Con had been celibate all that time…a man as virile as he was…was almost laughable. She only had to think back to the early days of their relationship, when the two of them had needed to do little more than catch each other's eye to want to make love. It should have been obvious to her that the fact that he didn't desire her any more was proof that he didn't love her, either.

She smiled sadly when she remembered the flustered expression on the young chamber-maid's face when she'd let herself in with her pass key to clean their room on the first day of their honeymoon…and the way she and Con had laughed helplessly when she'd hastily left again. She'd never been certain whether it had been the sight of their two naked bodies that had shocked the young woman so much or the fact that at some time during the night they'd joined the heap of bedclothes on the floor.

And it had always been that way between them, each taking joyous pleasure in the intimacies they shared, each as eager as the other for the next time they could be together, until...

Until the family they wanted to start didn't happen, and they were condemned to diaries and thermometers followed by nasal sprays and injections and endless indignities that had only resulted in more heartache than ever.

And somewhere along the line, the exciting spontaneity of their sex life had died with barely a whimper and taken their for-ever-after love with it.

No wonder she felt guilty now. How could she have been so selfishly wrapped up in her own misery that it had taken someone else to make her realise that Con wasn't happy with her any more?

Well, it might have taken her too long to see what had been happening right under her nose, but it had taken her only a few days to decide how best to deal with the situation. Con might not love her any more, but she still loved him enough to know that the only solution was to set him free.

'If only that meant that I could sleep better at night,' she grumbled softly as she climbed out of bed and padded to the door.

She glanced down at the oversized T-shirt that served as a nightdress and shrugged, doubting that there would be anybody about to see her disreputable nightwear while she warmed some milk in the kitchen.

Of course, she was wrong. Even in the gloom of the dark kitchen she could see that there was someone already sitting at the scrubbed wooden table.

'Jenna?' Callie said softly as she joined her, recognising one of their newer residents by the gleam of her pale hair. It had looked an unbecoming dirty grey when she'd turned up on their doorstep several days ago and had only shone with all its natural platinum glory after a long steamy hour spent locked in the bathroom.

'Hi,' she responded after a pause that went on

so long that Callie wondered whether the young woman would really prefer to be left alone. She obviously had serious issues to deal with and needed time to do it, but if it were that easy, her time on the street would surely have given her all the time she needed. The fact that she'd looked for a refuge must mean that either she was admitting that she needed help to survive physically, or that she needed input of another kind from people who had seen it all before.

Callie's own instincts told her to play a casual waiting game. There was no point in pushing for conversation if Jenna wasn't ready. It might even be counter-productive, driving her back into herself when she'd made the first move in reaching out to Marian at The Place to Go.

'I couldn't sleep,' Callie murmured as she padded across to the fridge and opened the door. 'Shall I make you some warm milk…or hot chocolate…while I'm doing one for myself?' she asked, hoping it seemed accidental when she turned to allow the light inside the fridge to fall across her silent companion.

The silvery gleam of tear tracks down her pale

cheeks made Callie want to wrap her in comforting arms but the way they were dashed away by furtive swipes of slender fingers told her that her sympathy wouldn't be welcomed.

'Chocolate would be nice,' Jenna agreed, before reaching for a sheet of kitchen towel and blowing her nose vigorously.

'There's a piece of Jodie's chocolate cake left, too,' Callie said as she removed the plastic box containing the remaining squares of the giant tray of it that she'd made that afternoon. They'd all cheered when she pointed out that she'd finally managed to fill them all when they couldn't manage to polish off something chocolaty.

Privately, Callie had thought that it was the rich buttery filling and the thick layer of chocolate decoration on the top that had made them all cry enough. The whole confection had been so rich that even the die-hard chocoholics had been satisfied.

'Comfort food,' Jenna said with a nod. 'That's what my mum calls it.'

'She's right,' Callie agreed, as she set two

plates down on the table and turned back to give the chocolate one last stir before carrying the two mugs over to join them. 'For some people it's a thick stew with dumplings all crusty and brown on the top, for others it's cheese on toast. What's yours?'

There was a pause and Callie was just starting to kick herself for trying to ask for more than the youngster was willing to give when she broke the silence.

'My mum's apple pie and custard,' she said with a hitch in her voice, and Callie could hear her swallowing against the threat of tears before she continued. 'She says it helps her to put things in order while she makes the pastry from scratch and peels and chops the apples. Then, while it's baking, she's stirring the custard till it thickens and she can let her brain get to work on the things that need sorting out so that when the pie comes out of the oven and she sits down to eat it, it can be a sort of celebration.' She picked at the square of cake, visible as a dark mass on the pale plate, but didn't taste any before she started speaking again.

'She made apple pie and custard lots of times after my dad died…while she was sorting things out in her head and at the bank and the mortgage company and when she was trying to get a better job so I would still be able to go to university.'

'And?' Callie prompted with her fingers crossed that she would continue. The poor girl obviously needed to unburden to someone, and if it would take the misery out of her eyes…

'And everything was starting to look as if it might work out when *this* happened,' she added grimly, with a gesture towards her noticeably thickened waistline.

Had her mother exploded when she'd found out? Had the father of her child dumped her as soon as she'd told him? There were so many questions she wanted to ask but Callie had a feeling that this was the time for patience.

'She'll be so disappointed in me,' Jenna sobbed suddenly, the words almost indecipherable as her misery overcame her. 'She's worked so h-hard so that I could stay at school and go on to college and I've gone and r-ruined everything. And Darren…he won't be qualified for two y-years…'

'So you haven't told either of them yet?' That much was obvious from the way she'd phrased it.

'I couldn't,' she wailed, for a moment forgetting that they were the only two awake at this hour. 'N-not till I'd decided what I was going to do.'

'Don't you think that they might be able to help you to come to a decision?' Callie suggested. 'Darren, especially. It's his baby, too, after all.'

The way Jenna sat there with her mouth open was enough to tell Callie that she hadn't even thought of that aspect, so she continued gently.

'I don't know exactly what the law is… Marian might… whether the father has a legal right to know about his child or not. But I would certainly think that he had a *moral* right to know that he's contributed to the existence of a new human being.'

'But—'

'That's just my personal opinion, Jenna,' she interrupted swiftly. 'Only *you* can decide which is the right way for you to go in this situation.' She had definitely said enough, and was now afraid that she might have made the youngster's problems even more complicated. After all, she'd never met any of the other people involved and had no idea how supportive they would be. To have any of the people she loved turn on her when she was feeling so vulnerable might just be the final straw for Jenna.

It was definitely time to lighten the atmosphere.

'It is also my personal opinion that this cake is possibly the most dangerous substance on earth,' she pronounced seriously. 'It's so delicious that you really don't care what it's doing to your waistline.'

'What waistline?' Jenna said with an unexpected grin as she took a huge bite.

'It's all right for you—you've got an excuse for getting bigger,' Callie complained as she picked up her own generous square. 'I'm certain that I've put on pounds since Jodie arrived...but at this time of night, who cares!'

After Marian's concern that she was losing weight, she had been conscientious about eating properly and for the first time in her life—apart from when she'd been pregnant—she had actually put on a little too much weight. She would just have to put in a few more hours of hard graft in the garden to work it off, she decided as the two of them crept silently towards their respective beds once their surreptitious chocolate treat was finished.

And in those solitary hours while she fought her battle with years of perennial weeds, she would have to face up to her own situation in the same way she advised the girls.

No matter how fulfilling she was finding her work here, she was never going to be satisfied until…until she finally found a bit of backbone…until she took her head out of the sand…until…

There were so many phrases she could use but they all came down to one thing. She was going to have to make contact, soon, because she couldn't live in limbo any longer.

A picture popped into her head of Con with the willowy blonde nurse and she didn't know whether to laugh or cry. She'd been such an emotional mess after she'd lost their son that she'd barely managed to hold herself together. Had her refusal to admit that she had postnatal depression really driven him into the younger woman's arms?

But what if it had been a lie?

It certainly didn't sound like anything the Con she knew would do. Had she been guilty of believing that he would do such a thing when he'd been completely innocent...completely faithful to their vows?

Either way, would he be willing to talk to her...to explore the possibility of taking her back? She didn't know, and hiding out at The Place to Go wasn't the place to find out.

She missed Con, desperately, and loved him so much that...well, that she'd be willing to agree to almost anything to have him back in her life. And even if that *anything* included more harrowing attempts at IVF, or searching for someone willing to be a surrogate to carry their child, or even exploring the possibilities of adoption...any of those options was better than a life without Con in it.

CHAPTER SEVEN

'I POURED you a coffee,' Sonja said as she stepped unnecessarily close to Con to offer the steaming mug.

He barely glanced in her direction as he turned the offer down, concentrating on the mechanics of tying his tie while trying not to remember that it was the one that Callie had given to him on his last birthday, nor the risqué use they'd put it to that night while he'd thanked her for her thoughtful gift.

He should have chosen another tie so that he wouldn't be ambushed by the memories, but he'd decided to wear his steel-grey shirt this morning for their weekly staff meeting and knew that the tie had been bought specifically to go with the shirt. Just because Callie wasn't there to appreciate the fact that he was wearing her gift, it didn't mean that he shouldn't take care of the way he looked, especially when he knew how much care she'd put into choosing the expensive slubbed silk.

'You'll need some caffeine before you start today,' Sonja said, as persistent as a wasp at his side. 'The board is already almost full. We're going to be at full stretch by the time the rush-hour accidents start arriving.'

'Staff Nurse Heggarty, when I want a cup of coffee, I'll—'

'Sonja,' she interrupted with a wide white smile, leaning so close to him that she was actually pressing her considerable breasts against his arm. 'We've been working so closely together for so long that it must be OK to call each other by first names…Connor,' she simpered up at him.

'My name is *not* Connor,' he snapped crossly, taking a hasty step away from her. What on earth had got into the woman?

'Con, then,' she corrected herself hastily as she closed the distance between them again, and Con suddenly had a picture in his head of a black widow spider approaching its prey and shivered when she continued speaking. 'I know you must have noticed how well the two of us work together…' She looked up at him under eyelashes laden with mascara and licked her lips suggestively. 'There's something special between us…something…'

'What on earth are you talking about?' he demanded harshly, wondering just how dim he'd been if she felt free to approach him so blatantly. 'You're a member of A and E nursing staff. Everyone in the department works well together.'

'But not as well as *we* do,' she insisted with a confident toss of her hair. 'There's a special magic between us…something far more than a doctor and nurse relationship…something that's been growing ever since the two of us met, and—'

'No,' Con said firmly as he picked her clutching hand off his arm with two fingers and held it away from himself as though it were a piece of noxious garbage. 'There is *nothing*—'

'You can't just deny it and hope it will go away,' she interrupted tenaciously. 'It's the sort of magic that could last a lifetime.'

'Stop right there, Nurse Heggarty,' he barked. 'You know very well that I'm a married man and it may be an old-fashioned ideal, but I would never break my vows.'

'But it won't be breaking your vows when you're divorced,' she pointed out persuasively. 'Then you'll finally have the chance—*we'll* finally have the chance—to have the children we want to make a *real* family.'

Con didn't think he'd ever met such a self-centred woman in his life. She was certainly the one with the least idea of what another person was thinking and feeling or she'd never have persuaded herself that he'd ever allow her to take Callie's place in *any* capacity, and certainly not as his wife.

It was only that morning that he'd surfaced from a fitful doze still wrapped in the lingering threads of a sexy dream and had turned over to pull Callie into his arms. The cold and empty space in the bed had been enough to remind him that the woman who meant everything to him had simply disappeared.

He hadn't slept properly in weeks…months if

he counted all the time since they'd lost their precious son and he'd lain awake listening to Callie sobbing out her misery and knowing that he could do nothing to comfort her.

'Nurse Heggarty,' he grated viciously, all the anger and fear and misery of so many days worrying about Callie finally boiling over. 'I don't know where you're picking up your gossip, but it's a pack of lies. My wife and I are *not* divorcing, and furthermore—'

'Oh, you don't have to worry about Callie,' she interrupted blithely. 'The two of us had a little chat about it before she left and she understands that you want someone who'll be able to give you the children she can't.'

The thought that Callie would discuss their marriage with Sonja was so laughable that he dismissed it instantly, but the fact that she'd dared to say it served to feed his anger, sending it roaring out of control and removing all brakes from his tongue.

'For your information, Nurse, in the unlikely event that my wife and I were to divorce some time in the next millennium, a...a...' For a moment he was lost for words until Martin's derogatory phrase suddenly leapt into his head. 'A yo-yo knickers like you would be the very *last* person I would ever turn to. You're not even fit for her to wipe her feet on.'

For just a second there was an awful feeling of satisfaction in seeing the woman's face grow white with shock, her artfully applied blusher becoming ugly terra-cotta patches on her pale cheeks. There was no simpering smile on that garishly painted mouth, now hanging slack and open, and the layers of mascara were starting to dribble down her cheeks with the swift rain of ready tears.

'I think you've probably said enough, Con,' Selina muttered as she appeared from nowhere at his elbow, for the first time looking less than her usual immaculate self, as though she'd thrown her suit jacket on in a hurry. 'Staff Nurse Heggarty and I will go to my office for a little talk. It would probably be a good idea if you went along to the coffee-shop in the main reception area for a coffee before you have to go to the staff meeting.'

Her calm, matter-of-fact voice and manner were enough to make Con feel thoroughly ashamed of his outburst. For all her personal problems, Sonja had the makings of an excellent nurse, but when he opened his mouth to try to find some sort of apology Selina shook her head and led the sobbing young woman out.

Con thrust his fingers through his hair and gripped a handful, wondering if pulling it out would make him feel any better. He'd had no right to take his feelings out on the nurse, no matter how annoying she was. She hadn't deserved to be so comprehensively demolished like that.

He took a couple of steps in the direction of the A and E manager's office then thought better of it. He didn't see himself as one of those men who could cope with women in floods of tears. He would follow Selina's advice about taking himself off for some coffee and save his apology for later.

It wasn't until he was gazing blankly out of the plate-glass window at the cheerful blooms massed in a row of planters that Sonja's ridiculous words came back to him. *'She understands that you want someone who'll be able to give you the children she can't,'* she'd said.

Could it be true? Had Callie discussed their marriage with the young nurse? 'Not likely!' he scoffed under his breath. Callie had barely spoken about her thoughts and feelings to *him*, let alone spilling them to someone who was little more than a stranger. As for any sort of agreement between the two of them to play pass-the-parcel with him… That was utterly ludicrous.

Wasn't it?

The more he thought about the crazy idea, the more sense it seemed to make, especially knowing how fragile Callie's emotions had been after their precious baby had died. He had recognised that she had been battling depression but whenever he'd tried to mention it, she'd told him she was coping. Had he believed her because he'd wanted to, not realising just how deep the depression had gone?

Could she *really* have sunk so far that she'd believed he wanted to replace her with someone who could give him the child that she hadn't been able to?

Had that been why she'd left him that message to set divorce proceedings in process…why she'd taken off with little more than her toothbrush and disappeared?

He closed his eyes and sighed heavily, wondering if he was finally going mad. He must be if he was really starting to think that his sane, sensible Callie would calmly step aside for someone like Sonja Heggarty to take her place to give him a child. She *must* know that a child would only be a bonus…the icing on the wonderful rich cake of their relationship. Surely he hadn't given her any reason to doubt that *she* was the most important person in his world?

His mobile phone shrilled, startling him out of his agonised introspection.

'Con, mate, have you got a minute?' asked Martin, and even over the phone Con could hear the edge to his voice.

'You've heard from her!' he said without a second's hesitation. 'Where is she? What did she say? When is—?'

'Hang on!' his old friend interrupted with a

touch of exasperation. 'I haven't spoken to her yet, but she left a message with my secretary to say she'll be ringing me this evening.'

'What time?' Con demanded eagerly. 'I could be with you by—'

'Hang on!' he said again. 'She's my client and until she specifically tells me that I can pass on information about—'

'She's only your client if you act for her in a divorce, but as there isn't going to *be* a divorce…'

'You're hair-splitting, Con,' he countered. 'You know that I'm bound by rules, every bit as much as you are in *your* job.'

'Dammit, Martin!' he exploded, completely forgetting where he was in his frustration. He only realised just how many faces were turned in his direction when the security guard stationed at the main entrance began to walk purposefully towards him.

'Sorry!' he mouthed as he held up his ID badge so that the man could see it, uncomfortably aware that a flush of embarrassment was reddening his face.

Once he saw the man turn back to his post he

hunched his shoulders and presented his back to the rest of the room.

'Tell me, Martin,' he said firmly, keeping his volume under control this time. 'Just tell me what time she's going to phone. Tell me so I can be there because I *need* to know that she's all right. If not, I'm going to go completely mad.'

Callie stood with her hand resting on the phone and waited for her pulse to slow down a little.

What an anticlimax, she groaned silently. She'd been dreading making that call, dreading learning that the papers were only waiting for her signature to end her marriage to Con, and the only person she'd been able to speak to had been Martin's self-important secretary—the one Con was convinced had firmly set her sights on marrying her boss.

At least she wouldn't have to speak to the woman again when she phoned Martin that evening, but she was going to have to steel herself to make the call…if her nerves could stand it.

In the meantime, she had a car full of teenagers waiting to go for antenatal check-ups. Thank goodness Marian had been able to arrange for them to go as a group, otherwise they could probably have filled a week with journeys to and fro one at a time.

'Will we have time to do any shopping?' demanded one of the girls, and when the rest eagerly chimed in, Callie had the feeling that they hadn't been sitting idle the last few minutes while she'd been making her wasted call, but had been using it to plot.

'It depends how long we spend at the antenatal clinic,' she said calmly, hiding her grin at the knowledge that she and Marian had known that this would happen and had made their arrangements accordingly.

Callie's only regret was that she wouldn't be there for Marian when the latest bureaucrat arrived later that morning to make yet another inspection of the accommodation. Would the journey towards securing official approval and funding never end?

'So, before we set off, has everyone remembered their record cards and their samples?'

'Yes, Callie,' they chorused like a well-trained class of six-year-olds, then burst into giggles.

Callie gave up on getting much sense out of them. She recognised that part of the hilarity was a reaction to nerves, knowing that the progress of their pregnancies would be under scrutiny shortly. The rest of it was a totally normal girlish glee at being out as a group, and the transformation in some of the girls since they'd arrived was almost unbelievable.

Of course, there were some whose journey to this point had been so traumatic that it was little wonder that they were withdrawn and hostile, but most of them seemed to have blossomed under Marian's welcoming acceptance.

Most were also willing to abide by the rules of the house, the major one being the total ban on the taking of any illegal drugs. She pressed her lips together against the sigh that wanted to escape when she remembered last night's confrontation with one of the newest residents.

Katy had openly admitted that she'd been using heroin but had claimed to have stopped several weeks ago for the sake of her baby.

Callie had had her doubts from the start. She didn't have to be a qualified doctor to see the signs that the girl was coming down from a high and she had been sitting in her room, still fully clothed, when she'd heard the sound of furtive footsteps.

Just in case it had been one of the other girls having to make one of their interminable trips to the bathroom, she had waited to see if the lock clicked on the bathroom door. When she'd heard the now familiar creaks of the staircase instead, she'd decided to follow.

It could still have been someone with what the girls called a bad case of the munchies, slipping down to find something to eat, the way she and Debs had not long ago, so she padded silently along to catch a glimpse.

Her heart sank when she saw the shadowy figure bypass the kitchen door and head straight for the cramped room that served as Marian's office.

'What does she think she'll find in there?' Callie breathed as she set off in pursuit, carefully missing each of the three steps that made the most noise so that she reached the ground floor with hardly a sound.

She knew—as did the rest of the girls in the house—that Marian didn't keep anything more than over-the-counter painkillers on hand, so there were certainly no drugs to find. 'And there certainly isn't any money to steal,' she muttered under the cover of the muted sounds of a hasty search. There was barely enough in Marian's dwindling kitty to pay the grocery bill each week, if the truth be known. Charitable status and funding couldn't come soon enough.

She'd just reached the door and was preparing to push it open and confront the girl when the desk light was switched on.

'Looking for something, Katy?' Marian asked sweetly, as the light caught the intruder full in the face, and Callie realised that the older woman must have had her suspicions, too, to have been sitting waiting in the dark like this.

Katy turned to run and found Callie standing in the doorway. 'Or did you just lose your way to the bathroom?' she asked with more than a touch of sarcasm.

Like a cornered rat, Katy bared her teeth, her hands tightened into fists.

'Very clever,' she sneered. 'But you both know damn well what I want, and I knew it had to be in here somewhere.'

'Money?' Marian asked. 'I'm afraid there isn't much. It's too close to the end of the month, when my husband's widow's support pension comes out.'

The girl swore coarsely. 'I could earn enough for a fix in five minutes against a wall—until I got pregnant—but there aren't many johns who want to do it to you when you're this far up the duff.'

'But I don't have any drugs here,' Marian pointed out. 'Nothing more than aspirin or ibuprofen.'

'*You* might not but *she* does,' Katy said with a flick of her dreadlocked head in Callie's direction. 'I looked in her room when she was down in the kitchen having a cosy chat with Debs and her bag wasn't there, so it *must* be in here somewhere.'

Callie ignored the fact that her privacy had been invaded—she hadn't brought anything of value away with her apart from a treasured photo of Con. She'd even cut up her credit cards in case she was mugged. The last thing she wanted was for their joint account to be emptied as a result of her decision to leave.

At the moment, her prime concern was Katy and she was tempted to cry at the waste of a young life. The girl was obviously intelligent enough to use logic, but hadn't realised that she was missing a few of the important facts.

'Sorry, Katy,' she said simply, 'but you're completely out of luck. No bag in here or anywhere in the house.'

'But…there's *got* to be. You're a doctor, aren't you? I heard the other muppets talking about you.'

'I'm a doctor, yes, but I'm not a GP. I usually work in an accident and emergency department, so the only sort of bag I carry around with me has my sandwiches in it when I take a packed lunch.'

Over the next few minutes, she and Marian had both tried to persuade Katy to stay with them—promised that they'd do everything they could to help her come off the drugs—but she wasn't interested. She wouldn't even agree to stay the rest of the night but stormed up to her room to grab her meagre belongings and stalked off into the night.

'Perhaps she'll come back?' Marian said hopefully as the two of them made their disheartened way back up to bed. 'After all, when she arrived she had no idea you were living here, so it wasn't the possibility of easy access to drugs that brought her here in the first place.'

'Perhaps,' Callie agreed, but she doubted it. Katy would probably feel that she had lost too much face by being caught trying to steal from them, and the fact that she'd lied about her ongoing drug abuse when there was an absolute house rule against it both counted against ever seeing her again. 'But, Marian, you'll never be able to save them all,' she reminded gently, 'no matter how much *you* want to, they have to want it, too.'

'True,' she said with a wry face, then grinned. 'But that doesn't mean I should stop trying.'

And with this group of girls, at least, it looked as if she was succeeding.

She had a car full of girls who were all clean,

in both senses of the word, and the ones who had joined them since she and Steph had were a long way from the sullen, distrustful and de-spairing people they had been. In fact, apart from the fact that some of them were heavily pregnant, they looked just like any other group of teenagers off on an outing.

'Hey, you lot, I've been doing some maths,' announced one of the girls. 'Do you realise that by the time we're Callie's age, we could be grandmothers?'

For some reason, this sent them all off into peals of laughter, but Callie wasn't amused. There was something heartbreaking about the fact that they had all become pregnant so easily...so casually...and that some were even planning to give their babies up for adoption, while she...

'I hope you won't,' she said quietly. 'I hope you'll tell your children how much you had to change your lives because they were on the way, and how you had to find somewhere to stay with strangers, instead of starting your family with a loving husband at your side to help you through the hard bits.'

'Yeah, well, things aren't done the same these days, you know,' an edgy voice said in the back, its owner probably unaware of how defensive she sounded. 'Us girls don't have to wait around for Mr Right to turn up. We got the same choices as the boys and can go with Mr Right-for-now.'

'The trouble with *that* is that men can't get pregnant and women can,' Callie pointed out sharply as she drove up and down, fruitlessly looking for a parking space. It might have been quicker to walk. 'After a night with Miss Right-for-now, men don't end up going through nine months of pregnancy, hours of childbirth and then eighteen years of trying to keep a roof over the child's head and food in its stomach.'

'Well, that goes to prove that God can't have been a woman, or She'd have made things fairer,' announced Jodie, who was only along for the ride. 'Perhaps She'd have made the men carry the babies, like seahorses do?'

Callie bit her lip as she manoeuvred into a cramped space next to an enormous four-by-four, cross with herself for sounding off like that. If there was any group of girls who knew at first hand the pitfalls of unprotected or promiscuous sex, it was this one. She was just grateful that Jodie's comment had taken the conversation off in another direction. For the rest of the day, she was going to have to make certain that her stress over speaking to Martin tonight didn't spill over again.

'Callie,' Marian called over the banisters that evening just as she was about to slip into the office to make her call. 'Could you come upstairs, please? And bring the bucket from under the kitchen sink with you…quickly!' she added as Callie heard the unmistakable sound of someone losing their supper.

'Has someone gone into labour?' she muttered as she grabbed the plastic bucket and set off at a run. Some women's first indication that they were about to give birth was an attack of nausea.

Except none of the girls was particularly close to their delivery dates and the obstetrician hadn't seemed unduly worried about any of them going into labour any time soon.

By the time she reached the top of the stairs it wasn't just one of the girls being sick but three of them, and the others all looked pretty green. This was going to be a logistical nightmare with only one working toilet on this floor so far. The plumber hadn't finished installing the other bathrooms yet, because they were still waiting for some essential fittings, and there was only one bucket.

'It wasn't my cooking, was it?' Jodie asked with a stricken expression on her green-tinged face.

'It couldn't be,' Callie reassured her. 'It's not long since we had supper, so it's too soon for our stomachs to reject it if there was something wrong with it. It must have been that Chinese take-away you all scoffed in the food hall of the shopping centre.'

'You told us you didn't like the look of the place,' Kylie said miserably as she wrapped both arms around the wastepaper basket that Marian had hastily lined with a plastic bag. 'You said there must be something wrong with it if it was the only quiet place in the middle of such a busy food court, but we didn't want to wait in a long queue.'

Callie followed suit, constructing makeshift buckets and handing the last one over just in time for the next stomach to reject the suspect food.

She was thankful that she hadn't eaten any of the take-away food, especially when two of the girls showed signs of increasing dehydration but were unable to keep even a few sips of water down. She would definitely be notifying the environmental health department in the morning.

'Marian, will you be all right if I leave you with the rest of them?' she murmured as they held a council of war in the corridor. 'Only I'd feel much better if I took these two in to be hooked up to drips. It's not good for them or their babies to be in such a state.'

'I'll be fine,' she said calmly. 'Just make sure you take the buckets with you. Oh, and remind the girls about the house rule…anyone who's sick in my car has to clean it up.'

It was more than an hour after they were admitted before Callie felt comfortable about leaving her charges in the antenatal end of the obs and gyn department, the two of them having been admitted to a shared room for an overnight stay, but it wasn't until she was passing the row of public telephones in the main hospital foyer that she remembered the phone call that had been haunting her all day.

'Martin, I'm so sorry to disturb you at this hour,' she apologised as soon as he answered. 'I know it's much too late to talk now, but I wanted to set up another time to—'

'Now is fine, Callie,' he soothed, sounding not the least bit sleepy when she was so exhausted she just wanted to collapse in a heap. It felt as though she hadn't slept properly for years.... 'You told my secretary that you wanted to speak to me, so fire away.'

'Well, um...' Now that the time had finally come, her mind had gone blank. All day she'd been trying to compose sentences in her head, needing to know if Con had confided in his friend, needing to know if Martin thought there might be a chance for her to undo the damage she'd done to her marriage. She'd been trying not to think about the possibility that Sonja had been telling nothing less than the truth. Con was the only man she'd ever loved and she'd been a fool to leave that way and she needed to speak to him to find out—

'Have you been in touch with Con yet?' Martin asked, and his words were so close to what she wanted to say that her carefully chosen words scattered.

'N-no. Why?' That was the last question she'd expected, but she should have, with Con being Martin's long-time friend.

'You ought to,' Martin said bluntly. 'Whether you decide to divorce or not, the two of you need to sit down together and talk.'

She had a sudden image of the two of them facing each other across a table full of papers while they dismantled nearly ten years of marriage, and her courage wavered.

'Shall I tell him how to get in contact with you?' Martin suggested, as though it were the easiest, most logical step.

'No!' she squeaked hastily, then swallowed and tried to sound a bit calmer, even though her pulse was suddenly galloping at nearly twice the normal speed. 'I—I'll get in contact with him in…in a little while…in a few days…' When she'd found some extra-strength starch to give herself some backbone and a top-notch script-writer to help her find the words she needed. If she told Martin where Con could contact her, she wouldn't put it past him to simply turn up on the doorstep whether she was ready or not. He'd never been the sort of person to sit idly by when there was something he wanted. He cer-tainly hadn't let any grass grow under his feet when he'd decided to ask her out, or when he'd proposed just four weeks later.

'If…if you really think it's the best thing to do, I'll contact him and…and suggest a meeting.'

'So, when shall I tell him that you'll be in touch?' Martin asked, his ordered mind clearly not liking the idea of leaving any loose ends. 'You've found somewhere to stay where you are? Somewhere safe?'

'Yes. I found somewhere good,' she reassured him, touched that he would be concerned about her safety.

'And you're well?' he prompted gently, and she nearly lost her tenuous hold on her emotions.

'As they say in all the best hospital bulletins, as well as can be expected,' she managed, swallowing hard to keep the tears at bay. 'Martin…thanks for being such a good friend,' she said hurriedly. 'I'll be in touch.'

'Promise?' he demanded. 'There are too few really good friends in the world to afford to lose any of them.'

Callie was too choked to say anything more, the enormity of the next step she was going to have to take quite overwhelming.

It would all be worth it if she and Con found a way to patch things together, but if they did end up in the divorce courts, she couldn't bear to think of all the things she would lose with the end of her marriage…her job, her home, her friends, but most of all the man who'd been the centre of her universe from the day she'd met him.

CHAPTER EIGHT

'HAND the phone over,' Con demanded gruffly. He'd barely held on to his control while Martin had been speaking to Callie, but that had been the price he'd promised to pay for being allowed to be in the room when she called.

'Con…' Martin actually hesitated, as though severely tempted to renege on his agreement, but Con wasn't having it. This might be his only chance to find out where Callie had gone, and he wasn't going to lose it because his friend was having a crisis of conscience over client confidentiality.

He reached out to relieve him deftly of the instrument and then it was the work of seconds to tap out the code to retrieve the phone number that the call had come from. His heart was beating as though it wanted to leap out of his throat and he found himself holding his breath while he waited for the information.

He was holding it again when he dialled the number he was given and let it ring...and ring...

He was just about to hang up and try again, convinced that he must have misdialled, when someone picked the phone up.

'Royal Infirmary,' said a male voice, and jealousy roared through him for a crazy moment before the words made sense.

'*Which* Royal Infirmary is that?' he asked, wondering just how many there were through-out the country. It had been a popular name when Victorian philanthropists had been building hospitals all over the place.

He was shocked when he found out exactly how far Callie had been willing to travel to get away from him. That phone call had come from the other end of the country, at least six hours of solid motorway driving away.

'Can you tell me, please, which number I have to ring to get in contact with a member of staff?' Con insisted with new determination. If Callie was working at the Royal he would soon know which department she was working in, and then it would be a simple matter of turning up and explaining…

An hour later, he was no closer to finding out where Callie was and he was quickly reaching explosion point, not least because his imagination had gone into overdrive, conjuring up all sorts of life-threatening illnesses that had necessitated her presence at the Royal, rather than that she might simply be working there.

'It's no good,' he conceded when he finally ran out of ideas and options and slumped disconsolately into the corner of Martin's settee.

It wasn't enough that the human resources department wasn't open at this time of night, but he'd also run up against someone who seemed to have swallowed the rule book about maintaining employee confidentiality.

'You'll just have to wait until she contacts me again,' his friend suggested. 'She'll have to give me an address if she wants me to send her any paperwork.'

'There isn't going to *be* any paperwork to

send her,' Con growled. 'And if you think I'm just going to twiddle my thumbs— No,' he said suddenly, leaping to his feet with his decision made. 'There's only one thing to do. I'll have to take a leave of absence from St Mark's and go and look for her.'

'What?' Martin yelped in disbelief. 'You're mad! What are you going to do when you get there—drive around all day until you spot her by accident?'

'I don't know, Martin,' Con admitted honestly as he fished his keys out of his pocket. 'I only know that I *will* go mad if I have to stay here, knowing she's up there. I haven't really got any option but to go and look for her if I want her back.'

'Dammit, man,' Martin muttered, then sighed. 'I suppose there's no point in trying to change your mind, so…keep in touch, please. I don't want to lose both of you. And you never know, she might get in contact with me again when she can't get you at home.'

'I'll have my mobile phone with me,' Con promised, his mind already moving onto thoughts of grabbing a change of clothes and a toothbrush. If he needed anything more than that, he could always buy it when he got there. The only thing he really *had* to do before he left was to notify the hospital that he was going to be away…although how long for, he had no idea.

You're wasting your time, you're wasting your time. Martin's voice echoed in his ears in time with the wipers as he drove the endless miles through the darkness, but he ignored it. It didn't matter…nothing mattered other than the fact that he finally felt as if he were doing something concrete to find the woman he loved.

There were only two things he wouldn't allow himself to think about…the first was not finding Callie, which wasn't an option because he didn't intend stopping looking until he *did* find her. The second was that when he found her, she might not want to come home with him, but that was the stuff of nightmares. He couldn't imagine his life without Callie in it…in fact, he refused to even consider the possibility.

He was almost dead on his feet when he finally turned into the main entrance to the

Royal Infirmary and when he saw the sprawling extent of the car parks, every one apparently completely full of cars, he was sorely tempted to avail himself of the first free corner he came to. Only the knowledge that he might be responsible for obstructing an incoming emergency vehicle made him obey the rules to spend a frustrating half an hour searching for a legitimate space.

Then, when he finally walked through the automatic glass doors and into the main reception area, he suddenly realised that he had no idea what to do next.

'How *do* you start searching for someone in a place like this?' he muttered as he stood in the middle of the open space while the rest of the world eddied around him.

The huge department guide on one wall was no help. Where was the point in knowing how to get to all the different departments if he didn't know which one Callie might be working in? At least during the long journey he'd managed to talk himself out of his panicky conviction that she was here as a patient.

'Can I help you, sir?' said a middle-aged man in the uniform of a security guard. 'Do you know which department you need to go to?'

'Unfortunately, no,' Con admitted, his brain sluggish with exhaustion. 'I'm actually trying to get in contact with someone. What would be the best way of finding out which department they're in?'

'Is this person a patient, sir?' his inquisitor asked politely, and everything froze inside him for a moment at the thought that Callie might be injured…even seriously ill. Then he remembered the fact that she'd been well enough to speak to Martin last night and dismissed the idea as the result of his tiredness and over-stretched nerves.

'No. A member of staff,' he said, with more confidence than he felt.

'In which case, I should try the human resources department, sir,' he suggested. 'If the person you're looking for is working here, they would have to know.'

Except the person Con spoke to couldn't have been less helpful.

'I'm sorry, sir,' she said stiffly. 'It doesn't matter if she *is* your wife. We are not allowed to give out information about our employees. It is against hospital policy.' The words were delivered as robotically as if they had been programmed into her on a computer chip.

The frustrating part about it was that it was the end of the month and the programme running on the computer in the corner of the department was probably processing all the employees' salaries while he stood there.

Well, short of doing some sort of action-hero leap over the counter and trying to access the employee records, he seemed to have hit an insurmountable block…until he remembered the telephone number from Callie's call last night.

He barely managed to wait until he was outside the main building before he dialled it from his mobile.

Once more it took a long time before the call was answered, this time by someone with a very young-sounding voice.

'Hello?' It was so hesitant that Con knew it wasn't a member of the security team.

'Hello.' He deliberately tried to smile, knowing that it would make his voice sound friendlier. 'Can you tell me where you are?'

'In the hospital,' he answered, clearly startled by the question, then wariness took over. 'Why do you want to know?'

'I only want to know where the telephone is,' Con explained quickly, afraid the youngster would remember all the stranger-danger talks at school and put the phone down on him. 'I've lost my wife in the hospital and she phoned me from that phone.'

'Oh.' He was silent for a moment, clearly thinking the matter over before he came to a decision. 'Well, it's in the accident place, where they fix broken arms.' And the receiver was replaced with a hurried clatter.

Minutes later, Con stood in the entrance to the accident department where his first quick look around made him feel almost as if he'd never left St Mark's.

There were the same serried ranks of chairs with their burden of suffering humanity and the same harried staff trying to cope with them while exhaustion dogged their every move. As ever, he wished that the bureaucrats who tried to dictate the best way of running such a department could be forced to spend time actually working in one. That way they might actually understand the extreme stress that being permanently short-staffed created.

Was Callie one of those staff? he wondered as his eyes searched from one passing face to another.

'Can I help you, sir?' asked a pleasant-faced woman in the pale blue cotton trouser-and-tunic outfit with the navy detailing that seemed to be the uniform for most of the staff in the department. Idly, he wondered whether the person who had chosen it realised just how much it resembled the crumpled scrubs that so many of them ended up wearing behind the scenes. 'Have you been through Triage or are you waiting for a patient?'

'Actually, I'm looking for my wife,' he announced, as he fished his wallet out of his pocket and flipped it open to one of his favourite photos of Callie…a photo that had travelled with him wherever he went ever since it had been taken, with her smiling face surrounded by wind-blown dark hair against a backdrop of the rugged Cornish coast where they'd spent their first impoverished holiday together. Ironically, it had been that holiday when they'd first decided to throw the birth-control pills away and start their family.

He dragged his eyes away from her smile, so full of joy at the thought that she would soon be pregnant.

'Do you work with her?' he asked, showing her the photo in a sudden decision to take the bull by the horns, because the sooner someone told him where Callie was working, the sooner she would be back where she belonged—in his arms.

'Oh, she's not a patient, then.' The woman glanced briefly at the photo and immediately began to shake her head, only to pause and frown, bending forward to take a closer look.

'She doesn't work in this department…unless she's very new and our shifts haven't crossed so far,' she said. 'But there *is* something familiar about her…'

Con's heart began to beat a little faster.

'You think she might be working in another department and have been called down to one of the patients?' he suggested, hoping to jog her memory.

'Perhaps.' She sounded doubtful and he could see that there were questions piling up behind her eyes, so he wasn't surprised when she challenged, 'So, how come you don't know which department she works in? You did say she's your wife?'

Loath as he was to speak about personal matters, this was probably one time when nothing but the truth would do.

'Yes, she's my wife. A trouble-maker at my own hospital told Callie that I was having an affair with her. I *wasn't*,' he stressed hurriedly, fiercely uncomfortable with baring his soul to a stranger, 'but Callie has recently lost our baby to a stillbirth and her emotions were chaotic, but before I could tell her it was all a lie, she disappeared.' He drew in a jagged breath, trying to forget just how long he'd been worrying and searching…and he still didn't know for certain that she was safe and well.

'So, why do you think she'd come here?' the woman asked warily. 'Is she originally from around this area?'

'No. We're both from the other end of the country, but when she phoned my friend yesterday, it was from the call booth over there, and I've driven all night to get here.' He rubbed his free hand over his face, only realising when twenty-four hours' worth of beard stubble rasped against his palm that he must look thoroughly disreputable. No wonder the woman wasn't very keen to help him.

Perhaps he should have booked himself into a B and B and had a shower and a shave before he began his search… but once he'd located the Royal Infirmary he hadn't been able to focus on anything other than the fact that Callie might be in this very building. After so many weeks, he hadn't been able to wait a moment longer to see her again.

'Do you want me to take the photo to the staff-room to see if anyone else recognises her?' the woman asked suddenly, and Con could have hugged her.

'Please,' he said, stupidly finding himself fighting tears.

'Get yourself a coffee while you're waiting,' she ordered sternly as he slid the precious photo out of its protective sleeve to hand it to her, and she pointed him in the direction of the coffee-shop that seemed to be run by the hospital volunteers. 'I've already got too many patients waiting for attention to have you collapsing all over my floor.'

It was nearly fifteen minutes of counting every second and the woman still hadn't returned, but at least the strong black coffee had given him a temporary boost.

As he'd sat there, he'd found himself playing the game he and Callie had shared…that of imagining far-fetched backgrounds for the other people around them. Callie had always had the wilder imagination and would probably have said that the nondescript middle-aged man dressed all in grey was an undercover spy when the truth was something far more prosaic…such as the fact that when he stood up it was possible to see that he was wearing a white clerical collar that probably meant he was a visiting chaplain of some denomination or other. Although Callie would immediately have insisted that he was still an undercover spy *pretending* to be a cleric.

The two young women were probably nothing more than they appeared, barely old enough to have left school, yet each with a toddler in tow and another one clearly on the way.

One little cherub with a mop of carroty curls grinned happily at him when she saw him watching her exploring her mother's handbag. When chubby little hands emerged clutching a bag of sweets the grin was even wider, and Con felt a familiar pang of loss that his own child would never have the chance to get up to such mischief.

The fit young man standing in the middle of the room wearing the striking bright green overalls couldn't be anything other than a paramedic. The word was emblazoned in reflective white letters across the width of his back as he turned in a circle, clearly looking for someone. It wasn't until Con saw that the man was holding a photograph in his hand that he realised that he might be looking for *him*.

'That's my photograph, I think,' he said, holding his hand out, depressed that the sympathetic nurse hadn't come to return it to him with some shred of good news.

'Maura said it's a photo of your wife,' he said, a clear challenge in his manner.

'Yes, it is. We've been married for nine... nearly ten years,' Con confirmed with an unexpected lift to his spirits when he realised that this was something more than idle curiosity. This man must have seen Callie and recognised her from the photo. 'When did you see her? Where?' he insisted bluntly, wishing they were somewhere a little more private than standing in the middle of a busy coffee-shop.

As if he'd suddenly realised that they were attracting attention, too, Mike—the patch with his name embroidered on it was attached right over his heart—beckoned him to follow.

In spite of the fact that he was eager to hear what the man had to say, Con couldn't help looking back for one last glimpse of that beautiful little girl with the cheeky grin, but there was no laughter in those sparkling blue eyes now. Instead, they were wildly staring in a terrified face as the toddler fought desperately for breath.

A couple of hasty strides took him back across the room, his eyes cataloguing everything in those fractions of a second to compare the possibility of anaphylactic shock due to an artificial colorant in one of the sweets with the probability of that forbidden sweet lodging in her throat.

'It's all right, sweetheart,' he soothed as he swung her off her feet and into his arms, automatically flipping her in mid-air so that she ended up face-down over his left arm.

'Here! What do you think you're doing?' screeched one of the young women as she lunged protectively towards her daughter, her chair legs scraping noisily on the tiled floor. 'You put my Tracey down!'

Luckily, her speed of movement was hampered by her pregnancy, allowing Con to deliver a firm thump between the struggling youngster's shoulder blades.

'Again!' ordered the paramedic as he crouched in front of the child, and this time when Con thumped he saw the offending sweet bounce onto the floor and under a nearby table.

'Ma-a-a!' the little girl was wailing even before Con could swing her upright, her face red now with indignation.

'Pervert!' the young mother shrieked as she snatched her daughter out of Con's grasp. 'Your sort should be locked up!'

'He saved your child's life,' the paramedic snapped as he bent to swipe up the sticky evidence with a paper napkin and thrust it under her nose. 'She had *this* stuck in her throat and couldn't breathe. If he hadn't acted as quickly as he did...'

'It's OK... Mike? Leave it,' Con said quietly, just glad that the child had suffered no lasting harm. Hopefully her young mother would be a little more vigilant in future 'We were in the middle of a conversation?'

Mike shrugged and turned away but Con could hear him muttering something about ingratitude as he led the way out of the coffee-shop and along the corridor towards the A and E department and the cramped little room that was obviously the paramedics' bolt-hole.

'Tea? Coffee?' he offered as he flicked the kettle on and gestured towards one of the rather battered-looking chairs that encircled a low table heavily marked with the circular evidence of many mugs slapped down urgently as the paramedics had hurried to the next callout.

'Nothing for me,' Con said, trying not to let his impatience show, especially in the face of the man's understandable wariness. For all he knew, Con could be a stalker trying to catch up with a victim who had fled to the other end of the country to escape him.

He spent the time while Mike was waiting for the kettle to boil in carefully replacing Callie's photo in the plastic sleeve that had protected it for so long and wondering just what he would have to do to convince the man that he was nothing more than what he seemed—a heart-sick man looking for his missing wife.

'Why have you come all this way looking

for her?' Mike demanded without any attempt at a preamble.

'Because she's my wife,' he answered simply, reticent as any man about discussing the emotions behind that fact.

'So?' Mike challenged face to face. 'If she's run away she must have had a damn good reason to come this far. Were you abusing her?'

'*Abusing her*…?' Con was stunned by even the suggestion. 'No! Absolutely not!'

'So what *was* the reason?' he challenged, and the tougher and more protective he acted the lighter Con's spirits grew, almost certain that it meant that not only had the man met Callie but he probably even knew where she was staying.

'A misunderstanding,' Con said cryptically, and wasn't really surprised when Mike snorted his disbelief, forcing him into giving a fuller explanation. 'Someone told her a pack of lies—that I wanted a divorce so I could marry someone who can give me children—and because she was depressed, she seems to have swallowed it hook, line and sinker.'

Mike was still regarding him warily and Con

suddenly realised that it wasn't going to do him much good to hang on to his pride or his privacy if he couldn't convince the man to help him. He hated the idea of baring his soul—the only person he'd ever trusted with his innermost thoughts and feelings was Callie.

'Listen, Callie and I have been through hell the last couple of years, going through IVF, and she was nearly full term with our baby when she realised that he'd stopped moving. She had to be induced for a stillbirth and has been breaking her heart about it ever since. She's been blaming herself, no matter what I say, so when this damn nurse told her that I wanted a family with her… She told Callie that I wanted a divorce when I've never wanted anything *less*.'

'Hell…!' Mike muttered, his wariness clearly replaced by sympathy, and that was the last straw for Con.

He was at the end of his tether, so desperately tired of all the weeks of uncertainty and so frightened for Callie's safety when she was in such a fragile physical and emotional state.

Suddenly, without any warning, his throat closed up and he was fighting tears.

'I didn't know she'd lost a baby,' the burly paramedic muttered with a dawning look of comprehension. 'That would explain why she ended up with Marian, then.'

'Marian?' For a moment it was as if Mike was speaking a foreign language as Con fought to make sense of what he'd said. Then he saw the silent battle the man was having with himself and could have groaned aloud. This was not the time for him to have an attack of conscience, not when he'd come so close to telling him what he needed to know.

'*Please*, Mike,' he said, not caring in the least if he sounded as if he was begging. He'd gone way beyond that now. 'I've spent so long not knowing if she was even alive. I need to find her…to see her…to be certain that she's safe and well. Please, tell me who Marian is and where I can find her. If she knows where Callie is…'

'She's safe,' Mike said in the sort of soothing tones that went with his profession. 'I think she's been staying with Marian ever since the mugging.'

'*Mugging*? Callie was *mugged*?' Con exclaimed in horror. 'When? How badly was she hurt? Did she—'

'Hey! Slow down!' Mike said, but Con was beyond soothing until he continued. 'Callie's OK, man. She just came to somebody else's help when *they* were mugged, and that's when I met her.'

It would take a little while for Con's pulse to return to normal, but in the meantime, there were other questions that needed answering.

'So who is Marian and where does she fit into things?' he demanded impatiently.

'Marian's a lady who lost her daughter a little while ago. I don't know all the details, but word is that she ran away with someone she met on an internet chat line, ended up pregnant and because she wasn't going for any antenatal care, didn't know anything about the symptoms of pre-eclampsia. She was already in full-blown eclampsia by the time she got to hospital.'

Con could remember a similar case a couple

of years ago. Callie had been distraught when she'd seen the tiny premature baby they'd managed to deliver by emergency Caesarean, knowing that, even if she beat the odds and survived, she would never know her mother.

'Anyway,' Mike continued. 'Marian decided that this area needed some sort of refuge for girls like her daughter, where they would be taken care of and helped through their pregnancy and those early weeks with their new babies. It's not officially open yet, probably because the paperwork takes for ever, but I doubt that Marian would ever turn someone away because of that.'

'So, if this is the place I've got to go to, what's it called and where do I find it?' Con demanded, feeling as if he was about to burst out of his skin with anticipation.

'That's exactly what it's called,' the paramedic said, turning cryptic at the last moment when Con was counting on him spilling every last detail. 'If Marian has done what she intended, there should already be a flyer in almost every telephone kiosk for miles around, telling the youngsters how to get in contact.'

Con was halfway to the door before he remembered his manners.

'Hey, Mike, thanks,' he said. 'You'll never know how much this—'

'Forget it, man,' Mike interrupted with an understanding smile. 'Just go and get that phone number…and good luck.'

CHAPTER NINE

IN THE distance, Callie could hear the telephone ringing, but she was feeling so physically and mentally exhausted this morning that she could barely lift her head from the pillow. After an extended session in the garden, while she'd wondered if she'd ever see the flower-filled haven she and Con had been designing between them, she'd fallen asleep almost as soon as her head had touched the pillow.

It was the dream that had come to her once she'd fallen asleep that had destroyed her peace of mind. Dreams of the heady days when she and Con had first met and the realisation that he was everything she could ever want. Dreams of his whirlwind courtship and her absolute certainty that their marriage was going to be perfect. Dreams that had swiftly turned into nightmares as she'd been told that their baby was dead and then that Con didn't love her any more.

After that, she'd lain awake for a long time in the darkness while she'd tried to sort out fact from fiction and untangle all her emotions.

It must have been the early hours before she finally admitted that she'd made an enormous mistake when she'd walked out on her marriage like that.

Even if Con no longer loved her, they'd had nearly ten years together and had been through so much while they'd tried to persuade her faulty body to do what it had been designed for. Those reasons were enough to warrant a serious face-to-face discussion before they decided to draw a line under their marriage and move on.

But what if Sonja had lied?

Just the thought was enough to make her feel sick, and it had been the topic that she'd pondered longest and hardest during the night, trying to understand the woman's motive. Surely, it had been an enormous risk if she *had* been lying, because all it would have taken was a single conversation between Con and herself to expose it. Or had the blonde not been as empty-headed as she'd pretended? Had she recognised the emotional state Callie had been in and realised that she would automatically believe the worst and that she loved her husband enough to be willing to step aside without any damaging confrontation, only wanting him to be happy?

'How could I have been such an idiot?' she berated herself. 'All these weeks of misery, going so far away to let him get on with his new life…as if I didn't think he was worth fighting for.'

Filled with a new sense of resolve, she took advantage of the fact that everybody else seemed to have gone downstairs to dive into the bathroom. Maybe a session in the newly installed shower would make her feel a bit more alert.

'Callie?' a voice called up the stairs, just as she worked the shampoo into a thick lather. 'Callie? The phone! It's for you!' the voice shouted again, loud enough to wake the dead, but she couldn't go out of the bathroom like this. Whoever it was would have to wait till she was dried and dressed. If it was some sort of emergency, Marian would be hammering on the door soon enough.

It was nearly a quarter of an hour before she went down the stairs on strangely shaky legs and made her way to the kitchen, knowing that she needed to eat. Unfortunately, she knew of old that when she felt this tired, she sometimes found it difficult to face any food.

'You look a bit green,' Marian commented after an all-encompassing glance and reached out to put two pieces of bread in the toaster. 'Could you manage a cup of tea with this?'

Callie paused for a second to contemplate the idea and when her stomach gave a very un-ladylike rumble discovered that it was just what she needed.

'Please.' She smiled. 'You must be a mind-reader', she said as Steph bounced into the room.

'There was a phone call for you,' she announced. 'It was a man with a dead sexy voice. He wanted to know if you were here.'

'He asked for me by name?' Suddenly, Callie's heart was in her throat. 'Did…did he leave a message?'

'He asked if Callie Lowell was here and I said you were…but there was no message. Just that he'd catch up with you later,' she said dismissively as she ambled across to the fridge and took out a container of orange juice, her attitude to nutrition now completely focused on what would be best for her baby.

For Callie, those few words had the impact of a detonator. Her eyes might be idly following the girl but her brain was racing like a jet-propelled mouse on an exercise wheel.

Really, there was only one person who would be impatient enough to want to track her down, one person with the determination and drive to find out where she'd gone…and to come to confront her?

She shivered at the prospect but there was no real dread in it. Callie knew she need never fear the man she'd married, only the heartache he might bring with him. It had been weeks since she'd last seen him, driving away from their house for his next shift at St Mark's, and no matter how hard she'd tried, she'd barely managed to go for more than a few minutes without thinking about him...without missing him.

'Will you excuse me while I make a phone call?' she asked politely, needing to make sure that it wasn't just wishful thinking, that it *was* Con who had phoned and that he might even now be on his way to see her.

Five minutes later Martin had confirmed the fact that Con had taken leave of absence from St Mark's and had set off to drive north, but had absolutely no idea how he'd managed to find her phone number. Callie was so jittery by the end of the call that she barely managed to put the receiver back in its rest. How long did she have to pull herself together before he turned up? A day? Two at the most, knowing how stubborn he could be when he was determined to accomplish something.

'Well, Callie, you can't really have expected him to sit on his thumbs when you disappeared,' Martin had objected, his divided loyalties clear in his voice. 'He's been looking for you ever since you took off.'

A part of her had been thrilled to hear it, especially as she'd finally come to the decision that it was more than time that she spoke to him.

Part of her was seriously regretting that she'd ever left because, apart from the fact that she loved him as much as ever, it had been impossible to put him out of her thoughts for more than seconds at a time. He was so much a part of her that it had been like tearing a limb off to leave him, and she'd been bleeding to death ever since.

For weeks now she'd been sticking her head in the sand—desolate that Sonja might have been telling the truth—but the more rational side of her had argued that Con was too trustworthy, too straightforward and honest to start an affair in the first place, and as for deciding he wanted a divorce…well, if it *were* true, he certainly wouldn't have ducked his responsibility for informing her of his decision face to face. And now that she knew he was on his way…

'Callie?' said a hesitant voice from the doorway, and she had to put her own concerns to one side when she saw the uncertain expression on Steph's face. 'Can I talk to you, please?'

'Of course you can. Is it about anything in particular?'

The question was redundant, really, when the heavily pregnant youngster closed the office door. It was an absolute rule that when the office door was closed, no one was allowed to interrupt except in case of dire emergency.

'It's about the baby,' she said as she perched uncomfortably on the only chair there was room for in the cramped space. 'I've been thinking and thinking about what I want to do when it's born and...' She paused to bite her lip, stilling its quiver for a second or two before she continued. 'I love it so much and I want to keep it, but...but I know I can't look after it p-properly.'

The tell-tale hitch in her voice almost had Callie hurrying across to wrap the tormented youngster in comforting arms, but she had a feeling that would actually make the conversation harder for her. This was the most frighteningly adult decision she'd had to make in her young life and Callie owed it to her to allow her to do it on her own terms.

'That sounds as if you might have made a decision,' she prompted gently.

'Well, Marian said that there are always people who can't have babies of their own who are desperate to adopt, and that they would love it and give it a good home and…'

For a second Callie was seized with the mad urge to say, 'I'll have it,' but even as the thought flashed through her brain she knew it wasn't the answer to either of their problems. She and Con had never reached the stage where they'd discussed the possibility of adopting, both of them totally focused on IVF and the conception of their own child.

She knew now that Con was on his way to see her, but didn't yet know if he was coming to propose a reconciliation or… Either way, she couldn't make such a hasty offer to Steph without knowing what her own future held. If she was going to be on her own, she wouldn't be able to give Steph's baby what this child-woman wanted for it—a real family with two loving parents. And even if Con did want her to go back with him, she had no idea how willing he would be to accept a child who carried none of his genes.

'So,' Steph continued with a new air of determination, 'I've decided that I'm going to give it up for adoption, and I'm going to go back to school and pass my exams and then I'm going to get some qualifications so I can come back and help Marian look after all the other girls like me.'

Callie hoped that everything was going to be that straightforward and murmured encouraging words but at the same time wondered if she would ever have been able to give up a child. She would definitely be haunted by fears that the child would always feel a certain sense of abandonment or rejection, no matter how loving their new family was.

'You know you don't have to make a decision yet,' she reminded the youngster. 'You've still got a little while to go before the baby's born.'

'I know, but I won't be changing my mind, even when I see it after it's born,' she said quietly, somehow seeming older and more composed now that she'd put her decision into words. 'It wouldn't matter how much I loved it because I'm too young to get a good job and I haven't got any qualifications and I'd never be able to earn enough to look after it properly. It would have a miserable life with me.'

Callie thought that she was probably underestimating herself, but if that was what she honestly believed…

'Marian will know the right people to contact when the time comes,' she reassured her. 'They have a list of people just waiting for a baby… people who have been checked to make sure that they're suitable.'

'Perhaps it's a pity there aren't people checking up to make sure it's only the people who are suitable that *get* pregnant,' Steph suggested wryly. 'They certainly wouldn't have chosen any of us girls here.'

She seemed…relieved that she'd come to a decision about her baby and had taken herself off to join the others who were having a chatter-filled curtain-making session for one of the bedrooms. Callie was left sitting in the office, alone with her thoughts.

Initially, it was Steph's decision she was pondering. Could she have been so single-minded at the same age? Then she found herself wondering if adoption would be possible for her, even if she were divorced from Con.

There were plenty of other doctors who were single mums, she rationalised, the divorce rate among medical personnel being what it was. And although nothing could ever replace Con in her life, adopting a baby would certainly go some way towards filling the gaping hole that had been left in her by her baby's death.

But did she have the right to be so selfish? It certainly wasn't that she didn't think she would love the child, heart and soul, but, even if she were allowed to adopt, it would be in the knowledge that she would be bringing the child into a less than perfect situation. Girl or boy, it would never know the special bond with a loving, caring father—the sort of father that Con would have been if she could have given him the children he wanted.

'Here, Callie, get this inside you,' said Marian, breaking into her increasingly convoluted thoughts as she set the belated mug of tea and plate of toast beside her elbow on the desk. 'Steph told me she'd spoken to you and that you'd helped her to get everything straight in her head.'

'Actually, I hardly said a word,' Callie admitted. 'She'd essentially made her decision, but she definitely seemed easier once she'd told me.'

'And how about you?' Marian prompted gently. 'If you need a listening ear, I have two available and all the time in the world.'

That wasn't quite true. Callie had never met a harder-working woman in her life, able to turn her hand from being a labourer on such a major renovation project as this old house to dealing with narrow-minded paper-pushers to counselling confused teenagers, sometimes all three at once. And all this was combined with trying to keep up with a granddaughter who didn't understand the concept of doing anything slowly.

'You heard that Steph took a phone call for me this morning,' she said, and saw Marian fighting with her curiosity.

'I didn't think you'd told anyone where you were,' she said as she perched herself on the corner of the desk, clearly unconcerned that she might be crushing some of the piles of paperwork that filled it. 'Have you any idea who it was?'

'There were only two people it could have been, and I'd just spoken to one of them before Steph came in to talk.'

'So, the other possibility is…?' she prompted patiently.

'My husband. He said he'd catch up with me later,' Callie said, not certain whether to see the words as a threat or a promise. For the moment, it felt rather like waiting for the other shoe to drop—in this case, in the shape of Con turning up on the doorstep.

The thought that he might be bringing the divorce papers with him was firmly pushed right into the darkest corner of her mind.

'You're not surprised, are you?' Marian asked. 'You must have known he'd come after you, because of the baby if nothing else.'

Callie wondering just what made her friend so certain that Con would want to travel all this way to talk about the son they'd lost. He'd been no more eager than she had to open that raw wound once she'd come out of hospital.

The sharp peal of the front doorbell—a strident testament to Marian's determination to renovate the wind-up brass original—interrupted their conversation before she could ask.

'That's probably the plumber,' Marian said with a grin. 'I phoned him first thing this morning to tell him I'd sourced the last of the fittings we needed for the new bathrooms.'

'I'll let him in,' Callie volunteered. She continued speaking over her shoulder as she set off down the corridor. 'Then I'll do another hour in the office to file away all those invoices. I got them all in chronological order yesterday. Oh, and I finished filling in the latest batch of grant application forms, so you now have a choice— you can either check them over and sign them voluntarily, or I'll be forced to hunt you down and nail you to the chair until…'

She never finished the sentence, the words disappearing out of her head without a trace when she opened the door and found Con standing on the imposing front step, those un-forgettable blue eyes meeting hers with the same strange feeling of inevitability as on the first time they'd met.

It *was* Callie standing there in the open doorway.

After so long, wondering whether he was ever going to see her again, the relief was so great that for a moment Con wasn't certain that his legs would hold him up.

She'd been talking to someone in the house as she'd opened the door, her face animated, vivacious and smiling.

How long had it been since he'd seen that expression light up her face and put a sparkle in those soft grey eyes? Too long, he answered silently, agonising all over again whether it had been his fault that she'd found it impossible to come to terms with the loss of their child.

He'd tried everything he could think of.

He'd almost smothered her with concern and sympathy in the initial days after the stillbirth, trying to take the look of utter devastation out of her eyes. Then, when that hadn't worked, he'd wondered whether she would prefer a little more space while she came to terms with the disaster in her own way.

That one time his desire for her had outstripped his iron control, he'd honestly believed that she'd wanted their physical joining as much as he had. He'd hoped that she would see the act as a time-honoured reaffirmation of their love…proof of the fact that life continued.

In his initial euphoria he'd thought it had been the first step towards a resolution of the recent devastating events, and that things would eventually improve, even if it never completely returned to what it had been before.

Her silent tears had told him that he'd miscalculated badly, but he'd never dreamed that he'd been so insensitive to her feelings that it would drive her away completely.

As for divorce…well, that just wasn't going to happen, not without a fight. He couldn't honestly believe that it had only been the lies of that self-centred nurse that had made Callie disappear—surely she was far too level-headed to believe such nonsense. But the buxom blonde had obviously been the catalyst that had caused the situation to implode, otherwise he wouldn't be standing on a doorstep at the other end of the country after a search lasting too many agonising weeks to count.

'Callie,' he said simply, and because it was her name and she was standing right in front of him, it was the sweetest sound in the whole world.

Callie felt her eyes widen when she saw who was standing on the step.

Con! Already! Here in front of her…

How could she have forgotten the way he made her heart race at nothing more than the sight of him…those broad shoulders…how often had she rested her head there…those long legs…camouflaged in worn denim at the moment but it took nothing to remember the hair-roughened feel of them when they were twined with hers…those beautiful hands… clenched in tense fists at the moment but so skilful and gentle…and, oh, that beloved face…the lean planes and taut jaw, the dark brows arching over eyes so blue that they could lift her spirits on the dreariest day…

'Callie,' he said, and she could have wept when she heard the familiar husky sound of his voice for the first time in so long.

What was it about that slight burr that sent a shiver up her spine and melted her insides? It had been like that the very first time she'd heard it, as though something inside her had been created specifically to react to the sound of this man's voice.

'Con,' she said, but her voice was little more than a whisper. She was barely able to believe that he was actually standing there, so tall that those unforgettable blue eyes of his were looking straight into hers, even though she was a step higher than he was.

She certainly hadn't expected him to be there so soon. She'd barely had time to come to terms with the fact that he'd found out where she was. At least she'd thought she would have a day or two to prepare herself to face him.

'May I come in?' he asked, and she was surprised to feel a swift wash of colour sweep up her face. She'd been so busy looking at him that she hadn't even thought about inviting him into the house.

She hadn't blushed since the early days of their relationship, she reminded herself crossly, and that had been when she'd been coming to terms with the fact that one of the most sought-after junior doctors in the hospital had sought her out and asked her to come for a drink with him.

'O-of course,' she stammered, stepping back to swing the door wide, feeling as gauche as a teenager...in fact, worse than a teenager. Most of the girls she'd met since she came to this house were far more worldly-wise than she'd ever been at their age.

'Come in, Dr Lowell,' Marian invited cheerfully from the other end of the hallway. 'Callie, take him into the office. It's not ideal and it's not tidy but if you shut the door, at least you're guaranteed that you won't be interrupted by any of the girls. I'll bring a tray in a minute. Would you prefer tea of coffee?'

'Tea, please,' Con said, while Callie found

herself hanging on every word, absorbing the sounds like parched earth with the first drops of rain as he added, 'I feel as if I've been mainlining coffee for ever just to keep going.'

And it didn't look as if it had done him any good, Callie thought when she looked a little closer and recognised the changes that had taken place since she'd last seen him. He looked thinner. Had he been forgetting to stop for meal breaks? They were permanently short of staff so it was all too easy to do when the department was busy. And his face looked drawn and sombre…almost as though he'd forgotten how to smile. Not that she'd seen much evidence of his mischievous dimples in the weeks before she'd left.

With the knowledge that Marian would be following them in a matter of minutes, Callie felt as if she had a little breathing space to come to terms with the fact that Con was here, but suddenly she was impatient to speak to him…*really* speak to him, the way she should have before she'd run away from everything that mattered to her.

It had obviously been an exhausting drive, if his unshaven appearance was anything to go by. What was so urgent that he'd apparently dropped everything, including his responsibilities at the hospital, and come to confront her?

For just a moment her insecurities rose up in force, taunting her with the possibility that it might be the divorce papers that had brought him here, rather than a wish to see her.

'Here you are,' Marian announced cheerfully as she pushed the door open with one hip, de-railing that train of thought before it could pick up any speed. 'Two cups of tea and some of Jodie's flapjacks—she added cranberries and whole hazelnuts to this batch. And before I take my leave of you both, please, will you let me make my long-overdue apologies?'

'Apologies?' Con had that familiar little pleat between his eyebrows that meant he was trying to untangle a puzzle. 'I don't—'

'A couple of years ago, you and Callie tried to save my daughter when she came into St Mark's A and E in full-blown eclampsia.' Now that she'd deposited the tray her hands were twisted together in a physical demonstration of the emotions coiling inside her, but Callie knew that she needed to get this off her chest.

'The two of you managed to deliver my granddaughter by emergency Caesarean but because my daughter died, I ranted and screamed at you. It was my guilt speaking, of course,' she admitted candidly. 'If Lisa had been able to confide in me, I'd have made certain she had proper antenatal care and it would never have gone so disastrously wrong.'

'I remember her,' Con said, and Callie knew that he wasn't just mouthing platitudes. He really *did* remember the teenager because he'd agonised for a long time over whether they'd really done everything they could for her. It was one of the things she loved most about him— that he truly cared about his patients even though the high-pressure world of A and E wasn't really the place to form any sort of real relationship with them. 'I'm really sorry that we weren't able to—'

'Please, don't,' Marian interrupted. 'I know you did all you could. I knew it at the time, but

I was just so devastated that I'd lost her that I think I went a bit demented. And her baby was so premature that I couldn't believe she would survive.' She shook her head and Callie could see that even with the passage of time the memories could still make tears well in her eyes.

'In the space of one day it looked as if I'd lost everything,' she continued with a quaver in her voice. 'Lisa was all I had left of my husband, and when her baby died—which I thought was only a matter of time when I saw how pathetic she looked—I would have nothing left of my daughter, either.'

'But she didn't die,' Callie told Con, still amazed by the tenacity of the tiny scrap of humanity she'd seen in the incubator that day. 'She's nearly two now, and she's absolutely amazing…a wonderful little girl.'

'And I have the two of you to thank for that,' Marian said as she reached for each of their hands and held on for a moment. 'Oh, the special care unit worked miracles with Emmylou, but if the two of you hadn't done that emergency operation, she would have died before she was ever taken up those stairs and into their hands.'

She drew in a deep breath but there was an audible hitch in it even as she brought herself under control. 'I've said many a silent thank you for your skill that day,' she continued. 'I thanked Callie the day we met up, and I've been waiting every day since for you to arrive so I'd be able to thank you in person, too. Today is that day, so, from the bottom of my heart, I thank you for trying to save my daughter and for rescuing my granddaughter and giving her a chance to live.'

'You were that sure I'd come?' Con asked, clearly startled by her certainty.

'Of course,' Marian said simply. 'Because of the baby.'

Callie wondered if it would always feel as if a hand clenched tightly around her heart whenever he was mentioned.

'I told Marian about the baby…about the stillbirth,' Callie said, and her heart clenched anew when she saw the shadow of loss cross his face.

'Yes, I know about that,' Marian said, almost dismissively. 'But what about the one you're carrying now?'

CHAPTER TEN

CALLIE'S ears were filled with a strange hollow roaring sound as she swayed in her seat. She could almost feel the blood draining out of her head as she tried to focus on what Marian was saying.

'It *is* his baby, isn't it?' the motherly woman asked with a hint of a frown, her eyes flicking rapidly from one shocked face to the other as Callie tried to draw breath.

'But…but I'm *not* pregnant…I can't be…I haven't been sick…not once,' she said brokenly, even as a wondering hand crept over the slight swell that she'd thought of as a reminder of the child she'd lost.

Pregnant?

Dawning hope warred with fear as she finally dared to meet Con's stunned gaze.

How many times had she gone through this—

the ecstasy of believing that she was finally pregnant—only to have her dreams shattered when the tests had come back negative?

The fact that she might be pregnant was the very last thing she would have thought of. After all, she and Con had only made love once in all the time since she'd lost his son, and the chance of that resulting in a pregnancy when it had taken a high-powered battery of drugs and technology to achieve it the last time was…was impossible…totally unbelievable.

'Here,' Marian said after a brief rummage in one of the deep drawers under the desk. Briskly, she slapped a packet in Callie's hand. 'You go and make use of this so you'll know exactly where you stand.'

Callie dragged her gaze away from Con's, unable to bear the dawning excitement she could see in his eyes when it was so unlikely to be fulfilled, only to see the pregnancy testing kit in her hand.

She wondered exactly how many times she'd gone into a bathroom with one of these. Every time she'd been filled with the same mixture of dread and anticipation. Every time she'd felt sick. Every time she'd had trouble making herself walk through the door to…

'Go on,' Marian urged with an understanding smile. 'It doesn't work until you take it out of the packet and—'

'All right! All right! I'm going!' Callie muttered, as she hurried out of the room on shaky legs.

Waiting for sixty seconds was always the hardest part, she mused as she washed her hands and then deliberately rubbed in some almond-blossom scented hand cream… anything to keep her eyes off the little strip until the time was up.

And then it *was* up and she couldn't make herself look at it, not sure whether she could bear it if—*when*—it was negative…again…

'Well, of course it's going to be negative,' she muttered as tears stung her eyes, so that she couldn't even focus on the indicator strip for a moment. 'Although, knowing my luck, I'd be the person who finds out that they've finally become pregnant the *normal* way on the same day that their husband asks them to sign the divorce papers.'

'Don't talk to yourself,' Marian ordered from outside the door. 'Talk to *us*. Have you done it? What does it say?'

Callie took a deep breath and blinked to clear the threatening tears before she could focus, then had to blink again.

With her eyes fixed on the wand clutched in her shaking hand, she reached out and flipped the latch on the door.

'Con…' she whispered, as she tilted it just enough for the two people waiting outside the door to see the indicator strip without losing sight of it herself. She couldn't drag her eyes away…didn't dare to in case the colour changed and dashed her hopes again.

'Congratulations, both of you,' Marian murmured warmly as she wrapped an arm around each of them for a brief hug and then nudged them towards the limited privacy of the office. 'There's no need to ask if you're pleased. It's written all over your faces.'

'I can't believe it,' Callie whispered, unable to

drag her eyes away from the evidence, the tears now streaming down her face unchecked with the knowledge that she once more had Con's baby growing deep inside her.

'Well,' Marian said as she did a brisk about-turn, 'the two of you obviously need to have a private conversation, so I shall leave you in peace. If you like, Con, I'll introduce you to Emmylou when you've finished.'

She didn't wait for a reply as she whisked out of the door and closed it firmly behind her.

'An amazing woman,' Con said as he turned towards Callie with a totally bemused expression on his face. 'Is she always like that?'

'You mean, like a human whirlwind? Pretty much, unless one of the girls needs a listening ear, and then she's patience personified,' Callie said with a smile, then she noticed the way Con was looking at her and the smile wobbled a little.

She didn't know which she wanted to do more—throw herself into his arms or curl up in a terrified ball to wait for the moment when she lost *this* baby, too—so she distracted herself by pouring the tea, regardless of the fact that it would now be past its best.

Before she could pass it to him Con finally reached the end of his patience.

'Well, you obviously didn't know about the pregnancy, either, so why *did* you leave like that, Callie? How could you go without saying a word to me?'

'I left a note,' she pointed out defensively, remembering just how difficult it had been to write. The thought that he didn't love her any more had been too raw and new for her to be able to bear saying anything to him in person, especially when she had been having such a hard time coming to terms with the fact that she'd never be able to give him the child he wanted.

All she'd been able to think, at that point, had been that it would be the only way she *could* leave.

'You left a *note*!' he said in tones of disgust. 'You've written longer notes to warn me you were going to be late home because you were collecting the dry-cleaning! Don't you think that our years together…and all we've been through in that time…warranted some sort of conversation?'

'Please, Con…' She couldn't bear it if they were going to tear each other apart. That was another of the reasons she'd left the way she had—so that there would be no bitter recriminations about whose fault it was that everything had gone wrong for them.

'No, Callie. I want to know. I *need* to know,' he insisted with a harsh edge to his voice that she'd never heard before. 'I'd been tiptoeing around you for so long after…after the baby died…wishing I could do something to make it easier for you…waiting for you to come out of it in your own good time… And then, just like that…' he clicked his fingers '…you disappeared without a word.'

If the room had been any larger she was sure that he'd have been pacing backwards and forwards, but it still felt as if she was trapped in a cage with an angry leopard.

Should she have gone to a counsellor when he'd suggested it? If they'd had some help after she'd lost the baby, when the cracks had first started appearing…when Con hadn't even wanted to wrap his arms around her in their shared bed, let alone make love to her…

'So, what was it?' he demanded, interrupting her spiralling thoughts. 'Did you decide to cut your losses? *I* couldn't do anything more to help you have the child you wanted, so you went off to pastures new?'

'What?' Callie gasped open-mouthed at this blatant distortion of the facts. '*You* were the one who went off to pastures new, as you put it. Or don't you remember telling your little girlfriend that if only *I* wasn't hanging on to you, you could marry *her* and have the family you wanted.'

As if he were a puppet and somebody had just cut his strings, Con dropped into the nearby chair, apparently oblivious to the fact that it already held a stack of papers. He was clearly shocked, his face so pale that she wondered if he was ill, and it was only when she saw the way he was grinding his teeth that she realised he was now blazingly angry.

'Stupid woman!' he snarled and Callie blinked in surprise. This conversation wasn't going the way she'd expected at all.

'Who? Me or Sonja?'

'Both of you,' he snapped, leaping to his feet again to glare down at her. 'Sonja for thinking I'd be remotely interested in her and you...*you* for precisely the same reason!'

'But...' It was hard to grasp a single one of her whirling thoughts. When she'd left, she'd been so certain that she was doing the right thing...leaving so that Con, at least, could be happy. But as the time had gone on with nothing resolved between them, she'd had time to think and to realise just how foolish she'd been not to speak to him first.

'Oh, Callie, if only you'd spoken to me,' he said, almost as though he could read her thoughts, the new gentleness of his tone clearly at odds with the anger evident in his clenched fists. 'How could you not know that from the day I met you there has been no one else for me. *No one*,' he repeated with an edge of desperation. 'If you believe nothing else, please, believe that I have *never* been unfaithful to you.'

'But...' It was her turn to collapse into the chair behind Marian's desk—the only other one that there was room for in the cluttered little office—leaving the two of them staring at each other over the piles of paperwork. 'She said…Sonja Heggarty said that you and she…that you didn't love me any more and…and…when she pointed out that if I let you have the divorce you wanted, she could give you as many children as—'

'What on *earth* made you believe the stupid woman, Callie?' he exploded. 'The whole thing was a figment of her imagination. Surely you knew *me* better than that?'

'But…it seemed to fit,' she said miserably, unable to remember those days too clearly. Everything had been blurred and distant, distorted by the all-encompassing depression that had enveloped her with the realisation that she'd just lost her last hope of having Con's child. 'I knew you weren't happy—you were barely speaking to me any more, and as for any… anything else…'

He thrust his fingers through his hair in blatant exasperation and for a moment it looked as if he was going to pull it out by the handful.

'Damned if I do and damned if I don't,' he growled as he planted two fists on the desk, leaning forward until he almost loomed over her. 'You listen to me, Callie Lowell. I love you every bit as much as I always have…the way I will always love you until the day I die. It was gutting me to see you so unhappy day after day and to be able to do nothing about it.'

'But, you were hardly ever home,' she began. He didn't seem to hear, clearly determined to finish now he'd started.

'I didn't even dare to cuddle you after that night…the only time I made love with you after we lost the baby. You cried,' he whispered, clearly tormented by the memory. 'I'd just made love to you and you cried and I felt so guilty when I realised that you weren't ready for…for that. I'm sorry, I just couldn't help myself when I kissed you goodnight and you actually kissed me back. Really kissed me. You know it's never taken much for my hormones to kick into overdrive where you're concerned, and I honestly believed that you wanted—'

'No, Con. I *did* want you. *That* wasn't why I

cried,' she burst out, unable to leave him believing something so wrong for a single second longer. 'It wasn't because I didn't want to make love with you or because it was too soon. It was because you were so gentle and so loving and it was so beautiful and I was just so relieved that you still wanted *me*, even though I couldn't give you the child you wanted so much…'

'Bloody biology!' he swore with feeling, and took another swipe at his hair. 'I'm sure that if we weren't so programmed to reproduce we wouldn't have half the misunderstandings in the world. How could you *ever* believe that I'd only love you if you could have a baby for me?'

Those last few words seemed to echo around them and their gaze flew almost simultaneously to the wand lying forgotten on the teatray.

'Oh, Callie,' Con breathed into the sudden silence. 'Is it really possible? After all those months and months of drugs and…'

'Don't get your hopes up, Con, please!' Callie wailed as the terror finally overcame her. Now that the initial euphoria of the positive test had worn off, a more realistic pessimism was taking its place. 'There's no guarantee that I'll manage to carry this baby to full term, either. They were never able to tell us why…why the baby died last time.'

'That could be a good thing,' he suggested persuasively. 'That means it's more likely that it was one-off and far less likely to happen with any subsequent pregnancy.'

'But what if it happened again?' she whispered. 'I don't think I could bear it…to find out that the heart wasn't beating any more…to have to go through labour all over again, knowing that the baby was already…dead.'

'So, what would you rather do? Have an abortion?' he demanded, suddenly stony faced, and she gasped at the suggestion.

'No! Never!' She shrank back into Marian's chair, instinctively wrapping protective hands across her belly as she stared up at him in horror. It only took a moment for her to realise that he'd used shock tactics deliberately.

'Well, then, that leaves us with only one other option… we're just going to have to take it one day at a time, the same as every other parent does,' he said gently, and stepped around the desk to take her hands in his. He tugged until she came out of the chair and into his waiting arms. 'We'll wait and we'll worry our way through the rest of the pregnancy…together… But we'll also be making plans, so that when he or she arrives…probably late and probably at the most inconvenient moment in the middle of the night…we'll be ready and waiting with names already chosen and the nursery decorated and equipped and…'

There was a wealth of loving reassurance in every softly spoken word and it was only when she wrapped her arms around him that she felt the tension filling every inch of his powerful body.

'Con?' She lifted her head from its perfect resting place in the angle between shoulder and neck and peered up to find his face every bit as tear-streaked as her own. 'Con, what's the matter? What's wrong?'

'Nothing,' he said with a very unmanly sniff and a slightly shame-faced smile that barely hinted at his dimples. He tightened his arms around her again, one hand guiding her head back to the place that felt is if it had been made especially for her. 'You know I'm not much for using flowery language but…when you went missing, it felt as if you'd ripped my heart out and taken it with you. At this precise moment, with you in my arms, my heart's back where it belongs and there is absolutely nothing wrong in the whole wide world.'

Callie's heart felt as if it swelled to twice the size in her chest as she pressed her cheek against his, mingling their tears.

'And…the baby?' she ventured hesitantly. 'If—'

'*If* we have a baby,' he interrupted, stressing the word deliberately, 'then we'll count ourselves lucky. But even if we never have a little Lowell, we're still luckier than anyone else in the world because I've got you and you've got me and between us…' He drew in a shuddering breath before he could continue, lifting his head so that he could look down at her with blue eyes dark with fervour. 'Between us, we've got everything we need to cope with whatever life throws at us. Haven't we?'

There was heartbreaking uncertainty in that final question and Callie suddenly realised just how much she'd hurt Con. And she couldn't entirely blame her actions on postnatal depression. Part if it had been sheer stupidity on her part that she hadn't trusted the one person in the world whom she knew to be utterly trustworthy.

'Yes, Con. Everything we'll ever need,' she said firmly, and caught a glimpse of those tantalising dimples.

'That sounded very determined,' he said with a new gleam in those beautiful eyes.

'It was,' she confirmed, firmly putting the agonies of the last weeks behind her as she suddenly found herself wondering whether their child had inherited Con's blue-eyed gene or her grey one. And there were so many weeks to wait before she could find out. 'Oh, don't get me wrong, my love. I'm still terrified that something's going to go wrong with the pregnancy, and the closer it gets to the week when we lost… Well, I'll probably be a nervous wreck the whole way through, but with you beside me…'

'You'd better believe I'm going to be beside you, all the way,' he said, the words clearly a promise. 'And when the midwife finally puts our baby in your arms…'

Except, when the time came, it was Con who lifted the squirming, squalling, dark-haired newborn into her arms as they both cried, but this time they were tears of joy.

'Hello, Adam Lowell. Welcome to the world,' Callie murmured as she tried to catch her breath.

'He's beautiful, Callie,' Con whispered brokenly as he wrapped his arms around both of them, watching as she counted and examined each tiny toe and slender finger and marvelled at each miniature nail. 'He's healthy and whole and perfect and…and I couldn't love you more for everything you've gone through to get this far.'

'I didn't do any of it without help,' she pointed out, more than a little euphoric that all the waiting and worrying were nearly over. If she hadn't had Con beside her, bolstering her

courage with every shared look and caress…
'Don't forget, half of every cell in his body
comes from you.'

'I've always thought it a pity the men don't
have to give birth to their half of each baby,'
muttered the midwife darkly, and they all
laughed when Con winced at the thought.

Then the next contraction hit Callie with
wrenching power and she groaned aloud even
as she exulted that Adam's brother or sister was
about to join him in the world.

It was at least another half an hour before
Callie was settled into her own room with a
clear plastic bassinet on either side of her bed,
both of them empty.

'I can't take my eyes off them,' she whispered
from the security of Con's arms, the two of
them ensconced in a veritable nest of thick
pillows as she cradled a son in each arm.

'Look all you want,' Con said. 'They're not
going to disappear.'

'It just seems like a miracle…a wonderful,
impossible miracle,' she sniffed as tears threatened, marvelling at how perfectly identical each

was to the other. 'To go through so much and lose so much and then to have everything just…fall into place so easily…'

'It didn't feel so easy when you went missing,' he pointed out sombrely even as he concentrated on taking one of her precious bundles into the crook of his arm without releasing her with the other. 'I nearly went mad trying to find you.'

'I'm just so glad you wanted to.' Callie snuggled into his free arm, relishing the way he automatically tightened it around her. Since he'd brought her home, that seemed to happen with delicious frequency. 'Although Marian has been complaining ever since that I never got to finish sorting out the garden for her.'

'She'll just have to persuade someone else to take it on, now that she's finally got her funding. My wife isn't going missing any more. She's staying where she belongs—with me and the start of our fledgling family.'

'The start?' she laughed in disbelief. 'You don't actually believe that lightning will strike twice? The professor said how rare it was for someone with my problems to conceive naturally.'

'We did it once, and got a spare one, free,' Con pointed out with a smug grin that showed his dimples off to best effect. 'Perhaps we just need to practise a lot and cross our fingers that we'll strike it lucky again.'

'That won't be any hardship,' she said with a grin of her own, then winced when she tried to stretch up to steal a kiss and pulled a few sore muscles. 'But I might just need a week or two to recover first.'

'No smutty talk, you two,' chided Marian as she walked in with an enormous armful of flowers. 'I'm going to be asked for a full account of everything you said when I get back to The Place.'

'Marian!' Callie cried when she saw her friend standing in the doorway. 'What are you doing here? How did you get here so fast?'

'A bit of forward planning and a phone call from that delicious husband of yours to tell me when your waters broke,' she said with a grin, then added, 'Everyone sends their love, by the way, especially Emmylou, who wants to know when the babies can come and play with her.' She tiptoed across to gaze misty-eyed at the two bundles they were cradling. 'Which one is Adam and which is Zack?' she demanded. 'I love the fact you've given them completely different names—from opposite ends of the alphabet! Are they identical or fraternal? Oh, this is so exciting.

'Oh, Callie, he's beautiful,' she breathed when the blanket was peeled far enough away from Adam's face to get her first glimpse of him.

'Of course he is,' Callie said, cheerfully doting as she threw Con a teasing glance. 'They both are. After all, they both look exactly like their daddy.'

She saw the expression of deep contentment spread across her husband's face when she said it and was suddenly impatient for him to hear their sons use the word for the first time, too.

'So, tell me,' Marian demanded as she perched herself on the edge of the bed where she could speak to them without losing sight of either sleeping infant. 'Was it worth all the waiting and worrying?'

'Need you ask?' Callie said as she smiled up into Con's glittering blue eyes and knew she was where she was meant to be. 'We've been lucky enough to get everything we've ever wanted…and so much more.'

MEDICAL™

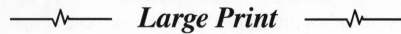

Large Print

Titles for the next six months…

December

SINGLE FATHER, WIFE NEEDED	Sarah Morgan
THE ITALIAN DOCTOR'S PERFECT FAMILY	Alison Roberts
A BABY OF THEIR OWN	Gill Sanderson
THE SURGEON AND THE SINGLE MUM	Lucy Clark
HIS VERY SPECIAL NURSE	Margaret McDonagh
THE SURGEON'S LONGED-FOR BRIDE	Emily Forbes

January

SINGLE DAD, OUTBACK WIFE	Amy Andrews
A WEDDING IN THE VILLAGE	Abigail Gordon
IN HIS ANGEL'S ARMS	Lynne Marshall
THE FRENCH DOCTOR'S MIDWIFE BRIDE	Fiona Lowe
A FATHER FOR HER SON	Rebecca Lang
THE SURGEON'S MARRIAGE PROPOSAL	Molly Evans

February

THE ITALIAN GP'S BRIDE	Kate Hardy
THE CONSULTANT'S ITALIAN KNIGHT	Maggie Kingsley
HER MAN OF HONOUR	Melanie Milburne
ONE SPECIAL NIGHT...	Margaret McDonagh
THE DOCTOR'S PREGNANCY SECRET	Leah Martyn
BRIDE FOR A SINGLE DAD	Laura Iding

MILLS & BOON®
Pure reading pleasure

1107 LP 2P P1 Medic

MEDICAL™

Large Print

March
THE SINGLE DAD'S MARRIAGE WISH Carol Marinelli
THE PLAYBOY DOCTOR'S PROPOSAL   Alison Roberts
THE CONSULTANT'S SURPRISE CHILD   Joanna Neil
DR FERRERO'S BABY SECRET   Jennifer Taylor
THEIR VERY SPECIAL CHILD   Dianne Drake
THE SURGEON'S RUNAWAY BRIDE   Olivia Gates

April
THE ITALIAN COUNT'S BABY   Amy Andrews
THE NURSE HE'S BEEN WAITING FOR   Meredith Webber
HIS LONG-AWAITED BRIDE   Jessica Matthews
A WOMAN TO BELONG TO   Fiona Lowe
WEDDING AT PELICAN BEACH   Emily Forbes
DR CAMPBELL'S SECRET SON   Anne Fraser

May
THE MAGIC OF CHRISTMAS   Sarah Morgan
THEIR LOST-AND-FOUND FAMILY   Marion Lennox
CHRISTMAS BRIDE-TO-BE   Alison Roberts
HIS CHRISTMAS PROPOSAL   Lucy Clark
BABY: FOUND AT CHRISTMAS   Laura Iding
THE DOCTOR'S PREGNANCY BOMBSHELL   Janice Lynn